VISION
OF
FOLDED-SPACE

KEITH RADMALL

Ordering Information:

Prime Seven Media
518 Landmann St.
Tomah City, WI 54660

Printed in the United States of America

Table of Contents

WAR

MY (COVID-19) THESIS

DEEP THRO@T !

As I throw my mind, I slowly look upon the crystal ball. Then as the haze within clears, this is what I saw. You are about to enter a world of your existence or is it ! Through-out this time line, from beginning to end you are about to have your belief that the planet earth exists, taken from your mind. If not swept away by impossible hope for humanity. Or by the wickedness that people can create an do. To the terrifying growth of the unknown. Where the terrifying truth has got so clear. That only end of days shows the way. Only your denial of what is said will reassure you that life on the planet earth is still possible. How this has come about you and only you can decide. Then I leave you with this... As the vastness of space is a beauty of its all. Who are you to say that you and only you decides what is and what is not.

SPACE

- First words spoken by Neil Armstrong when he became first human to step on the surface of another planet, the moon.

  "One small step for man, one giant leap for mankind".

Satellites #1

In 1959 from a British warship based in Australia the British empire launched the first satellite 200 miles of the coast of Solomon islands in the glorious month of November.

The war ship had the inept name HMS Empire.

Two months later the U.S.A. launched satellite Telstar from Cape Canaveral, I think the fuss was because it was not only there first satellite launch but also their first rocket success.

Two months later Russia launched lunar sputnik 1. Then the country of America strived to gain dominance in space. Where Russia thought screw that and left them in their wake. Concentrating the importance of mechanical skill. In 1970 China launched its first satellite into orbit called China 1 from Dangfanghong space centre. India launched its first satellite in 1980, Rohini RS 1 from Satish Dhawan space centre.

The first manned rocket was launched by Soviet Union on the fantastic date of 12.4.1961

The cosmonaut Yuri Gagarin on space ship Vostok 1 became first human to leave earth atmosphere. Alan Shepard in 1961 took flight in mercury 1 from Cape Canaveral an became first American in space.

Another fantastic achievement has to go to the Americans who flew in Apollo 11. Commander Neil Armstrong lunar module pilot, Buzz Aldrin lander of lunar module eagle and flight captain Michael Collins who flew the command module Columbia. Where on 20.7.1969 Buzz Aldrin and Neil Armstrong became the first humans to land on moon. Then to enhance the fact Neil Armstrong became first man to walk on moon.

The two space men spent 21 hours 36 minutes on the planet's surface.

In 1975 the first meeting in space between America astronauts and Russia cosmonauts when Apollo 9 and Soyuz 5 docked together over Europe.

P.S. Note : Now the space race begins who will be the first to hold the moon in its hands and possess its secrets to a further existence.

Satellites #2

Many countries around the world have launched satellites into space. If not being able to do it themselves they have achieved success with the aid of foreign space ports.

Legendary feats of success of satellites are

Voyager 1 launched September 5th 1977

As of January 2022 was 14.5 million miles from earth, has reached inter stellar space.

Voyager 2 launched August 20th 1977

As of February 2021, was over 11 billion miles from earth, has reached inter stellar space. Science have discovered so many wondrous things from these pioneering events. With each time they give an update it has been a joy to read and see. The science of NASA and others with their scientists should feel very honoured. Because it is an honour to hear what they say.

Hubble space telescope launched 24th April 1990 orbits planet earth at fifteen orbits per day.

It travels at a speed of five miles per second. The telescope was launched of space shuttle discovery... Its purpose to explore the universe in visible, ultraviolet and infrared wavelength. One of the most important science projects ever has found 40,000+ objects not visible from earth.

On 1st August 2009 Arian 5 rocket launched largest ever telecommunication satellite Tenestar from European space port in French Guinea. In July 2018 Space X launched heaviest ever satellite (15,600lb) Telstar 19V from space port at von horn, Texas, U.S.A.

P.S Note : No one knows where humanity is going in its space journey, but it is exciting to see.

Stations

The first platform in space was set up by USSR. Salyut 1 was set up in 1971 by the tragic space flight crew of Soyuz 11. Military stations of the Salyut Class were 2,3,5, also known as Almaz stations. There have been seven Salyut stations. Salyut 7 was lost in space February 1985. Last cosmonauts before the loss were Leonid Kizin, Vladimir Solvyov, Oleg Athou. Who all returned to earth safely. Russia successor to Salyut stations was station Mir. Which was operated by USSR then later Russia from 1986 to 2001. Crashed out of orbit 23.3. 2001. Skylab created by NASA existed in space for 24 weeks. From May 1973 to February 1974. It was operated by three separate three-astronaut crews Skylab 2, Skylab 3, Skylab 4. Crashed to earth in 1978. ISS international space station launched in year 2000. ISS has hosted most astronauts at one time that number being 13 and has been constantly maned. ISS is the biggest station in space, having add-ons over the years. There have been decommissioned space stations. U.S.S.R. Salyut's, Russia Mir, NASA Skylab China Tingong 1 and 2 in September 2011.

Shenghou 8 successfully performed automatic docking in November 2011.

Tiangong 1 crashed to earth on 2.4.2018

Tiangong 2 crashed to earth on 19.7. 2019 Tiagong space station in low earth orbit started launch up 29.4.2021.

P.S. Note : Are they stations to bring space to us or blockers stopping us reaching out to space !

Astronauts

1. Alan Bartlett Shepard Jr
   Space flight, 1961, 1971
   Walked on moon during second mission.
   Born 1923 Died 1998
2. Gus Grissom
   Space flight, 1961, 1965
   Born 1926, Died 1967
3. John Herschel Glenn Jr
   Space flight, 1962, 1998
   Born 1921, Died 2016
4. Scott Carpenter
   Space flight, 1962
   Born 1925, Died 2013
5. Gordon Cooper
   Space flight, 1963
   Born 1927, Died 2004
6. Wally Shirra
   Space flight, sigma 7 1962
   Born 1923, Died 2007
7. Deke Slayton
   Space flight, 1975
   Born 1924, Died 1993
8. James Benson Irwin
   Space flight, 1971 Apollo 15 pilot of lunar module walked on
   moon 3 days
   Born 1930, Died 1991

9. David Randolph Scott
    Space flight, Apollo 9 1966, Gemini, 1971
    Apollo 15 mission commander, first to drive a moon vehicle the
    moon rover on moon 3 days.
    Born 1932
10. Alfred Merrill Warden
    Space flight, 1971
    Apollo 15 pilot command module, Endeavour.
    Born 1932, Died 2020
11. Bruce McCandless
    Space flight, STS-41B, STS-31
    First ever untethered space walk
    Born 1937, Died 2017
12. Sally Kirsten Ride
    Space flight, 1983
    First American female in space.
    Born 1951, Died 2012

Cosmonauts

Yuri Alekseyevich Gagarin
Space flight, Vostok 1-1961-U.S.S.R
First human in space.
Born 1934, Died 1968

Gherman Stepanovich Titov
Space flight, Vostok 2-1961, Vorkhod 2-1961 U.S.S.R. 4th person in space.
Born 1935, Died 2000

Valentina Tereshkova
Space flight, Vostok 6-1963-U.S.S.R.
First woman in space
Born 1937

Valery Polyakov
Space flight, Soyuz TM-6 / 1988 TM-7, TM-10
Soyuz TM-18 / Mir TM-20,
On Soyuz TM-6 spent 88 days in orbit.
From TM-18 spent 437 days on Mir
Born 1942, Died 2022

Sergei Konstantinovich Kirkalev
Space flight, 6 missions
Stranded on Mir during colapse of U.S.S.R.
Spent 311 days in space
Born 1958

Yuri Pavlovich Gidzenko
Space flight, three missions
Lived on Mir and ISS stations
Born 1962

Svetlana Savitskaya
Space flight, Soyuz T-7 1982, Soyuz T-12 1984,
First woman to take a spacewalk - 1984
Born 1948

Aleksandr Volcov
Space flight, Soyuz TM-7, Soyuz TM-13,
Soyez TM-14, Twice on Mir space station
Born 1948

Taikonauts

Name : Yang Liwei
Flight : Shenzhou 5, 14 orbits
Date : 21.6.2003
Born : 1965

Name : Nie Haiseng
Flight : Shenzou 6, Shenzhou10, Shenzhou 12
Date : 12.10.2005, 11.6.2013, 17.6.2021
Born : 1964

Name : Fei Junlong
Flight : Shenzhou 6
Date : 12.10.2005
Born : 1965

Name : Zhai Zhigang
Flight : Shenzhou 7, Shenzhou 13
First Chinese space walk
Date : 25.9.2008, 15.10.2021
Born : 1966

Name : Lui Boming
Flight : Shenzhou 7, Shenzhou 12
Date : 25.9.2008. 17.9.2021
Born : 1966

Name : Jing Haipeng
Flight : Shenzhou 7, Shenzhou9, Shenzhou 11
Date : 25.9.2008, 16.6.2012, 17.6.2016
Born : 1966

Name : Liu Wang
Flight : Shenzhou 9, 1st Chinese woman
Date : 16.6.2012
Born : 1978

Name : Liu Yang
Flight : Shenzhou 9, Shenzhou 14
Date : 16.6.2012
Born : 1969

Name : Wang Yaping
Flight : Shenzhou 10, Shenzhou 13,
2nd Chinese woman in space,1st Chinese woman to spacewalk,
Date : 11.6.2013, 15.10.2021
Born : 1980

Name : Zhang Xiaoguang
Flight : Shenzhou 10
Date : 11.6.2013
Born : 1966

Name : Chen Dong
Flight : Shenzhou 11, Shenzhou 14
2 space walks, Tiangong station
Date : 7.10.2016, 6.10.2022
Born : 1978

Name : Tang Hongbo
Flight : Shenzhou 12
Date : 17.6.2021
Born : 1975

Name : Ye Gangfu
Flight : Shenzhou 13
Date : 15.10.2021
Born : 1980

Name : Cai Xuzhe
Flight : Shenzhou 14
Date : 5.6. 2022
Born : 1976

To date as of 2022 fourteen Chinese taikonauts have gone into space.

Species

A number of different live species have been honoured with a trip into outer space. A dog called Laika in 1957 on board sputnik-2 U.S.S.R became first animal to orbit planet earth. With sadness I must report it died in space. In 1949 a monkey named Albert II went and died in space. Of 71 dogs sent to space 17 have died. As of 2022 thirty-two monkeys have been in space.

1947 - fruit flies

1949 - monkey

1950 - mouse

1957 - dog

1961 - ape

1961 - guinea pig

1963 - cat

First animals in deep space & around moon

1970 - frog

1973 - fish

1973 - spiders

In 2007 European space agency mission foton-M3 exposed Tardigrades to ten days of open-space. With survival rate being 100%.

In 1975 on board Soyuz-20 tortoises spent ninety-one days in space. A record for animal space travel.

In 2012 mice spent 91 days on board ISS.

The longest time expanse at a space hotel for a non-human species.

The first animal to orbit planet earth and land successfully were two dogs Belka & Strelka of the soviet sputnik 5 mission series on 19.8.1960.

Other animals that have voyaged to space are bees, ants, newts, snails, butterflies, pigs, scorpions, cockroaches, crickets, moths, minnows, jellyfish and others.

Spacial

It is the year 2022 and the number of known people to have gone into space is 574 from 47 nationalities. 72 soviet cosmonauts and 49 Russia cosmonauts.

The number of people that have walked on the moon is twelve. The number of women who have been in space is seventy-five.

Eighteen people have lost their lives in space. With the two worst incidents being with North American Space Agency (NASA).

On 28th January 1968 challenger space shuttle blew up ending the lives of seven crew member. In 2003 seven astronauts were lost on the shuttle Columbia when it broke up on take off from Kennedy space centre. The remaining four incidents were with Russian cosmonauts. The first was cosmonaut Vladimir Komarov on 24th April 1967 when the parachute failed to open on landing on his Soyuz 1 capsule. In 1971 all three cosmonauts crew of Soyuz 11 mission were lost when capsule decompression happened before re-entry when on their way back from first ever stay at a space station, Salyut 1.

A further thirteen loses had been while training for space exploration. Of those loses there was on 27. 1. 1967 Apollo 1 astronaut Gus Grissom, Roger Chaffee (novice spaceman), and Ed White the first astronaut to take a space walk. During training for space mission while in a cabin fire broke out and took all three lives.

Space continuum

There are three main purposes for space exploration. They are Satellites for communicational and observation and Space ships for travel. There is also talk of habitation and mining. Examples of success space station, moon rocks.

In 2010 commercial space travel was created.

Definition tourism for human space travel for recreation purposes. Different types of space tourism are orbital, sub-orbital and lunar space tourism.

Space X launched first space tourist American Dennis Tito. Arriving at ISS for eight days departing earth 16.9.2021.

On 31.3.2022 Blue Origin launched six tourists into space. They are based at van horn space launch centre, Texas.

Space X using a falcon 9 rocket launched from Kennedy space centre 8.4.2022.

It carried retired astronaut and three civilians to ISS.

South African Mark Shuttleworth was a space tourist in 2002 with the Soyuz TM-34 mission to ISS. He spent ten days in space.

Commercial space travel has become a lucrative business venture. With people willing to pay a lot of money to get a glimpse of earth from the other side. It has also created a big advancement in space technology to accommodate space tourism in a short space of time. From the American Apollo series and the Russian Soyuz series we now have Virgin Atlantic, Space X, Blue Origin. Companies are paying large amounts of money to get there satellites launched into space. With the European space agency being the world leader in technological launch sequencing.

Technology for space exploration is a slow tedious outcome but with the creation of commercial space it has gotten to be a lot faster slow pace.

Throughout exploration in space fantastic inventions have been made such as the moon buggy that travelled on the moon. Space suits that have enabled humans to walk in space. Space material that can stand the pressure of re-entry into earth atmosphere. There is the NASA space shuttle that can piggy back a ride to the fringes of space then can go it alone and return from space like an aeroplane. Then there is the latest wonder a rocket that can go to space then return and reverse and land back on earth ready to refuel and go again.

Here in the year 2022 many countries now have the capabilities to make some form of advancement into outer space. With manned flights the ultimate quest. That success being with China, Russia, America.

P.S. Note : NASA launch operation centre (LOC) at Cape Canaveral renamed Kennedy Space Centre on 20th December 1963.

Space map

Okay listen up this is where we are heading.

Yay, where might that be? I don't know, some place called space. Now if the information my agents gave us is correct. We with another load of bits and bobs have been stuffed into what is called a milky way, and that is not the kind you rip open and eat. It is what you open and say would you like a bit. But looking at you, so much for that. The parts of the whole are in synchronization of said planets from earth to planet Pluto inclusive of said planets Moonies. O yes and the our known sunshine.

So what is about as we reach for space are ionic spheres and once we break out we enter into what is around. Then as you observe there is real estate in abundance such as planet Mars, Jupiter, Mercury, Neptune and others. There is also moons such as Titan that surround the planets, as you can see if you look upon in a wider expanse are surrounding.

Beyond the chocolate bar I mean the Milky Way is the outside known to land lubbers as the solar system what ever happened to the stratosphere. Where lost in space there are various galaxies. One of these known well is alpha censorious. Other is the cosmos.

The distance and magnitude of said space phenomena is so vast is why the discovery of hyper space travel is so important. The answer to this is keep learning to the good and discover from your mind's eye to distance make-up and improve upon. As space is infinite on mass is created by the abundance posset on a planet. Other degrees of magnitude are the creditability of meteors, comets and asteroids that roam space at their leisure. Just think with your mind anything is possible.

Engineering

A big thank you must be given to those men and women who devoted their experience and time to launch the space program. All the designers who were at the forefront of design fitting to go forth into space. Mathematicians that ensured exposure and diagnostics were correct for a safe and successful mission.

Mechanics whose precision was vital in putting the various satellites and space vehicles together. The ground staff at space command that helped the crews of spaceships when required and gave them reassurance, and whose importance it was to feed in start-up vision and stability process for satellite function. Also sponsors who were tireless in showing support for the endeavour. A massive thank you given by the devoted audience that caught a glimpse of the many amazing feats of various space exploits. Then there are the lesser known people from ancient times that envisioned and opened peoples mind to the vast unknown.

One such person was:

Aristotle, Born 384 BC., Died 322 BC.
Place of birth Stagria, Greece.
Recognised space as being finite.

Another person of note:

Edwin Powell Hubble,
Born 20.11.1889, Died 28.09.1953
Place of birth, U.S.A.
Was a pioneer in mapping space.

P.S. Note : May there persistence in deliverance guide them on to other things.

Space program #1

Mercury space program was America's first manned endeavour into space. There were six flights with six astronauts. The first flight was 5th May 1961. The last flight of the series was 15 th May1963. There were six flights in total, with space craft Freedom 7, Liberty Bell 7, Friendship 7, Aurora 7, Sigma 7, Faith 7.

Gemini NASA's second space program started with the launch of Gemini 1. on 8 th April 1964, then Gemini 2. 19 th January 1965. Both flights were unmanned. The Gemini series was launched in 1964 and ended in 1966. The missions were Gemini 1,2,3,4,5,6,6A,7,8,9,9A.

Sixteen pilots flew in the flight program. Gemini 9 crashed while manoeuvring on the ground with the loss of two astronauts during training. Gemini six failed mission to dock with Agena station (target / propulsion) when Agena station blew up and was replaced with Gemini 7.

Apollo space program launched in 1968 and finished in 1972, was the effort of America to put a man on the moon. There were eleven Apollo missions 1,7,8,10,11,12,13,14,15,16,17.

Apollo 7 was the first successful launch in the Apollo program on 11th October 1968.

Apollo 11 was the first successful landing on the moon in 1969.

Russian space program started by U.S.S.R. with launch of sputnik 1 in 1957 and ended with the collapse of U.S.S.R. with final forge into space being crewed flight Soyez TM-13 on 25. 12. 1991. The sputnik program continued throughout the reign of the U.S.S.R. and changed to the soyez program, which is continued as in Russia. The Russians have continued its space program with furthering its expertise at the international space station and exploration of space by spaceships and satellites. It is now seeing no use for the west so is preparing to leave the ISS.

Since the year 2000 commercial space tourism has tried to become established in space.

Space companies that have reached space with civilian crews are Virgin Galactic the first commercial space line. Space X founded in 2002 launching out of four different sites and Blue Origin formed in 2000. Virgin Galactica established in 2004 is based in California and launches from space port, New Mexico. There launch sequence is from a ride & drop from a Boeing 747.

Space X has a rocket launch pads at four centres in U.S.A.

1. Cape Canaveral
2. Vandenberg launch complex,
3. Brownville south Texas launch site.
4. Kennedy space centre.

Blue origin has a launch facility in west Texas in America, it is a sub-orbital complex.

Russia refrained from space tourism in 2010.

P.S. Many other countries are making claims to going to outer space. Well let me put that into perspective. It not only costs you tens of millions for the small part of, but it also cost you tens of billions for the bigger parts. So to reach and be in space a.k.a. conqueror and explorer it is a perfect example of a money pit.

Space program #2

There are different countries involved in space exploration. China started its space program under the guidance of China National Space Administration (CNSA) and China Manned Space Agency (CMSA). The Zhengzhou rocket launch program commenced in 1991.

With launch of rocket Zhengzhou 1 in 1991 and Zhengzhou 14 a manned launch on 5 th June 2022.

Their 9th manned flight into space.

China launched its first satellite in 1970

Dong Fang Hong 1. In 2019 China launched Chang'e 4 probe and landed on dark side of moon, the first to do so. A Tianwen-1 mission in May 2021 landed a probe on the surface of Mars. First space ship launch Zhengzhou 1 20 November 1999. First manned flight Zhengzhou 5, 15 October 2003. China space station started in April 2021. Will take eleven missions to complete.

European Space Agency (ESA) established on 14th April 1964 and has seventeen European member states. Headquarters Paris, France. Space port located in French Guiana, South America. Known as Guiana space centre or Europe space port. In operation since 1968, with first launch 1970. Number of launches 307. Uses the Ariana rocket. There have been no manned flights.

Japan Aerospace Exploration Agency (JAXA) established with first satellite launch in 1970.

India Research Space Organisation (IRSA) founded 15 August 1969. In 1980 ISRO launch first satellite RS-1 in India using rocket SLV-3 from spaceport Shar Centre Sriharikota, India.

P.S. Note :The list of countries that make claim to having a space program looks like an encyclopaedia of flags.

Space facts

- I am so spaced I don't know if I am coming or going

- Coming through make space

- If we make more space, we can put it there

- The space is so small

- The space is so big

- A spatial enmity, something you don't recognise or understand.

- If we space the objects like so it will be easier to circumnavigate

- Space is infinite

- What is wrong with you, are you spaced?

- Space time continuum, a life preserve in space

- As the rocket stopped in space, the planet told it where to go

- Pilot: Finally, I have the spaceship under control. Navigator: We are running out of fuel. Pilot: Are you insinuating I am full of hot air?

- Throughout time and space, the rest is to do

- I am so spaced, I am out of my head

- If you find a space we can set up there because this isn't do-able

- Use that space for that, put them there it should be fine

Spacoids

- Rocket: a mechanical contraption used to extend from one atmosphere to another.
- Satellite: a protector of a life desire of their wish.
- Space shuttle: a space ship with the ability to return to land as a plane.
- Space suit: the required clothing to travel in space.
- Space rover: a four wheeled vehicle capable of travel on another planet.
- Booster rocket: Gives extra thrust, gives required power to leave a planet's atmosphere.
- Astronomy: a map of outer space.
- Spatialized: experienced in all aspects of space travel.
- Space station: a fixed complex in space which serves a purpose.
- Astronomical: a reading of weights, measurements, distances and spectres in space.
- Capsule: a part of a space ship where crew can be kept alive while traveling in space. Can separate from rocket for controlled re-entry into planet atmosphere.
- Space-walk: when an astronaut leaves the capsule and is suspended in space.
- Spaceity: a certain aspect in the whole of space exploration.
- Planet rover: a mechanical object that annualizes a planet surface without human interjection. Information about terrain, take samples: dust, soil, rocks, liquid.
- Astronaut: someone who travels in space.
- Space log: A dialogue of endeavour to explore space.

Historical

Historical space pioneers are those that opened humanities eyes to the wonders outside our planet. Them and their small findings helped use to realise what we have now achieved.

Aristarchus born on island of Samos, Greece died Alexandria, Egypt. Was the first to claim that planet Earth orbits the Sun.

Galileo Galilei (1564-1642) from Italy was first to use newly discovered telescope to observe planets and stars. He also discovered that moon surface was not smooth.

Johannes Kepler (1571-1630) from Germany known for three laws of planetary motion.

Planets move in orbits shaped like an eclipse.

A line between a planet and sun covers equal areas in equal time.

Konstantin Eduardovich Tsiolkousky
(1857-1935) Russia.

Robert Esnault Pelterie
(1881-1957) France.

Herman Obreth
(1894-1989) Born, Romania Died, Germany.

Fritz von Opel
(1899-1971) Born, Germany Died, Switzerland.

Robert Hutchings Goddard
(1882-1945) United States of America
Pioneered astronautic theory.

Considered founding fathers of rocketry and astronautics.

Edwin Powell Hubble (1889-1953) U.S.A.
An influential astronomer of twentieth century.
Discovered in 1920s that other galaxies exist beside our own Milky Way Galaxy.

Wernher von Braun born 1912 in Poland, died 1977 in America. Head of NASA space flight program and put man on moon in July, 1969.

Isaac Newton (1643-1727) England.
His discovery of gravity was the main obstacle to create space travel. He contributed to the fields of gravity and motion. Newton's law of Universal gravitation.

Two objects attract each other with a force of gravitational attraction that's proportional to their masses and inversely proportional to the squares of the distance between their centres.

Newton's three laws of gravity

1. An object will not change its motion unless a force is acted on it.
2. The force on an object is equal to its mass times its acceleration.
3. When two objects interact they apply forces to each other of equal magnitude and opposite direction.

Mission

A space mission has different meanings. The best known is to put a human in space. The other is to put a human on the moon.

North American Space Agency (N.A.S.A.).

Mercury missions to explore space.

Gemini missions to put a man in space

Apollo missions to put a man on the moon.

Soviet space program former U.S.S.R. Established (1952 - 1991).

Sputnik missions to explore space and make ready for human exploration. Started the Soyuz space missions.

Russia space agency (ROSCOSMOS) established 1992, space flights, cosmonautics, space research. Soyuz space missions 14 and counting.

A rare but excellent space mission program has been developed by Europe.

European Space Research Organisation (ESRO). Established in 1964.

European Launcher Development Organisation (ELDO). Established in 1964

Used Europa rocket for seven missions.

European Space Agency (ESA).

The amalgamation of ESRO and ELDO.

Established in 1975.

Uses Ariana rockets for missions.

The ESA have not launched any manned missions. But have launched over 350 missions for research and satellites for communications & technology.

P.S. Note : The latest NASA mission the Artemis is a program to go to space, return to the moon and with success go further.

Space story

This story is my story about the space race. If my intelligence is correct this is how I won the space race. It has been close on seventy years since agents were sent to gain intelligence for my conquest.

Firstly do not believe the ancients, they're all drugged up. The coming of miriuoochie, you know how it is. In 1958 after hijacking a warship, you know how it was after the war back to counting the pennies. It was easy loading up the three trucks with spare parts a.k.a. left overs. Then H.M.S. Empire suddenly disappeared from the scrapyard. It was not going to be missed, the sea was awash with heraldic honour. Guards got paid off with excellently printed money, a.k.a. the other £75,000,000. Then after getting fed up while putting Sputnik together a.k.a. is that right satellite. While the others got drunk.

Then on the 4th great day of November 1959 a.k.a. when the bottles were empty. We all gave a great ooh as the decomposed 32 font gun launched the satellite into space. With just over seven mega tons of thrust.

Then after the first bottles were empty a.k.a. a sudden call up for military service the three good ones made the plans with great expertise that sent mercury one into lower orbit. The American space program finally got off the ground.

With great heartache with bottles empty and call up for military service the three great ones were thrown into outer space. With a capacity of 75,000 mega tons thrust.

Then with what was left really well happy for him the lot was drawn. Then with great wondrous honour the first a.k.a. bottle was emptied and landed to walk on the moon.

Then looking at nothing bottles all empty an so one last thrust I struggled with a.k.a. drinks coming out of the pub and last few days of military service. Booked my two friends into a taxi (all the way thinking their paying for it) and last moments of sobering up put them on an elevator. To (space ship) to hotel outside (Mir).

With endeavour and calculation I cannot imagine what the future holds.

P.S. Note : Because it is spaced!

P.S.S. Note : I could not understand why the two crews fried up on the space launch pad (ESA) in Guinea. All over it (by the skin of my teeth) I thought do not do it. It is too heavy, the rest is history. Lives should not be lost a new. Because everything has to be checked.

Spacey

I can't think much about space, I guess I've entered a void of voidance. They are just thoughts that I know are there.

They are abominable space, space anomaly and space bomb. I imagine if I think long enough I shall be able to break through the void. Then I shall know their true meaning.

I am going to create particle compound in my mind and see if I can catch their meaning as they drift fall from each particle section. Where everything before you is not what you expect to see. It does not fit right, the sense of senses are mixed with no understanding, the sound is of nothing, it is getting closer the further away seeing less keeps getting closer.

Creating something abominable. E.g. abominable space but the further I succeed the less I know what I am looking at. It is in my mind but it is not there in form, but it is space anomaly.

It is a quiet calm night as I look up into the night sky. They're closer than it has ever been, Haley's Comet up in the sky. Speeding by at a fast speed, with a heat aroura in its wake.

What does it look like a.k.a. space bomb.

P.S. Note : It does fit, because how would you be able to read it in sleep mode.

Space – line

- The ancients that opened up our mind to what is possible to achieve in outer space.
- The suppliers that made the equipment for expeditions to outer space
- The engineers that put the parts together to launch humanity into space.
- The unmanned rockets that showed the way to launch into space.
- The animals that showed it was possible for an organism to survive in space.
- The first manned space flight into lower orbit to ensure it was safe for humans.
- The first manned space flight to calculate longevity in space.
- The first unmanned rocket launch to the moon.
- The first unmanned landing and take-off on the moon.
- The first manned journey landing, steps and return from the moon.
- A first time human walk in space.
- The creation of an orbiting space station.
- The capability of rocket to dock and release from space station.
- The planners for further visits into space.
- Space control centre on planet earth that protects, guides and ensures a safe and successful journey.
- The people that write historically about space flight.
- The people that create toys to expand the mind about real space.
- Exhibits of what it is like in the expanse of outer space
- Photograph images of what space looks like.

P. S. Note : The rewards of space are slow in coming but they are of an immense significant.

Space bulletin

Today in the news from outer space is again a regular focus. Firstly I would like to talk about the amount of junk that is floating in space. That the earth gravity has not been able to get hold of and crush and burn. Still no agency has come forth with any kind of gesture to clear it out. Anyone would think they can afford what they do out there. On another common note, which is a failure to complete! With all the 'this that and the other' by said space programs. There are still many costly failures. Which I hope said novices and experts are being able to use to their advantages in the future. Yet again with the talk about this and that failures are beginning to slow human success in exploring space. On a lighter note various satellites are sending back outstanding photos of the far reaches of space. Not to mention close encounters. Example aligning of planets, Stars and planets being closest ever.

Techno lodge seems to be racing ahead, on paper anyway. But it is important to resolve before you deploy. Because it can affect the program exponentially in time and cost. I know you are very google eyed at the amount of money you can make, but I hope you find time to take into consideration your devoted and loyal fans that follow you and find great enjoyment in making you famous in the world masses.

P.S. Note : This is an observer for a space bulletin waiting to receive your next exciting message from outer space.

Universal space

I am now beginning to be a part and float in a sense off space. If my intelligence is right I shall soon be gone and the planet Earth will be a figment of my imagination. I don't know which has lifted my happiness sequence more. The corona virus outbreak or to be gone of this place, maybe both. The bustling moments of the past to growing of my mind through time, to my now present which I am endeavouring to make a part.

From the beginning of time I have attempted to share knowledge by phasing through the planets orbit of time... To the end of in my heart a fantastic moment in the universal continuum. To behold the final ending to the beginning. I have phased in what the human calls modern time from anti - matter space.

I have beheld the awesome rage of a universe denied. I have sensed the warning of truth told and what actions to take. I have sensed your foreboding of execution as you have seen in and energy surge of a pandemic.

The universe is a gracious heart of one meaning. That is to further the expansion of its being. Anything else is particle compound which in its eyes is nothing. What human eyes see as its ending.

P.S. Note : As I step from the pod I observe my surroundings. I see trees waving in the high breeze. I see an abundance of withering colour green, rising from the ground. I see flowers of angle dust set in abundance to explain where you can get off. As far as the eye can see I see a blazing sun the colour of green. Behind the pod is a raging river flowing that sparkles like diamonds. I'm thinking I could like this place, whatever that is as my eyes turn to the pod.

Edition

This is a unbiased view of the space race. When Britain launched beagle 1 into space in 1959. When it started transmitting it enabled digital communications from one end of the country to the other. With stereophonic capability across all of Britain and possibility of beyond.

On midnight January 1st 1960 beagle 2 was launched from twenty-five miles of the Shetlands coastline, again from HMS Empire.

When cresting on the extremity of space it sent out a signal of fifteen seconds saying U.S.A. is about to launch satellite Telstar.

As communications were lost it packed up, then burnt out returning to earth.

HMS Empire was then returned to the scrapyard and decommissioned.

Has the world laughed at the U.S.S.R. space program? With failure to launch one after another. They found success in putting first human in space which in quick procession brought more successes. With their mechanical technical expertise they saturated earth orbit with space techno lodge. Which enabled them to create space station and making claim to space exploration when asked about their space program. They also landed space probes on Moon, Mars and Venus. Meaning their space program is a technical acknowledgment to further their mechanical expertise in space.

The space program in U.S.A. was created on the knowledge of foreigners. Which took them to space and the glory of first human lander on the surface of another planet the Moon. But when the foreigner became of no use, their space program started to malfunction so they closed it down. After re-evaluation since it's ending in 2011. NASA is going to attempt to start again with the artimus program in 2022.

European space agency program is a fully fledged technological gift to outer space. In a more regretting phase losing two, three man crews that were burnt to death during countdown to launch into space. Where ended its human endurance in space.

China space program has been a rapid expanse into space from satellite to rocket to space man to space station. It has a deep space program. There is evidence it has used foreign techno ledge for its advancement.

P.S. Note : Countries are doing this

Space race

This is a short intel of rockets into space.

Russia : ROSCOSMOS
First to launch rocket
First to launch a satellite into space
First to send non-human to space
First to launch a human into space
First to land a probe on planet Venus
First to build a space station
First to dock at a space station

America : NASA
First to rocket to the moon
First to land on moon
First to walk on moon
First to eject from the moon to make rocket contact in space
and return to earth
First to land probe on the moon
First to land probe on mars

China : China national space agency : CNSA
Successful in satellite launch
Successful in launching rocket into space
Successful in sending rocket to to moon
Successful in building space station
Successful in docking at space station

European space agency : ESA

Highly qualified in sending rockets into space with satellite pay loads and making rocket parts for other nations.

P.S. Note : Propaganda say America is better at everything it dose. But mechanics of space say Russia. With a wink of an eye China has literally done it all, so who won the space race.

F.T. Note : A good rule is acquire an then check, then check with, then check with all.

Future space

Many thoughts of where humanity shall be in the future as they endeavour to conquer space.

From the insignificant words of ancients where words were considered silly and quickly forgotten. To space tourism for crazy money that most don't have. Since the end of the second world war when Russia and America devoured the German space technology Russia and America unleashed their powers of understanding to get an acknowledgment on how to live in space. Once near space was finally reached the space race slowed but was not stopped completely. Then in the new millennium technology stepped forward and a new space race began. With the advocacy of private money it has got the space race now going past the moon to mars. Many new ideas which are, I think, old ideas dressed in bling, have been put forward on paper at least. I think these people that are paying for it are beginning to realise the cost of cheap extravagance that is over in days.

Putting the cost aside this preference on space (my thoughts) as to change. Meaning the chain reaction to locate, stabilize, survive, must be on set. Then if the capabilities to transport and live on another planet can be focused on. To obtain this satisfaction it is first paramount to get control of space rocket movement. Then the satisfaction of change to can be seen and done safely. When developing movement in an unknown it must not be infringed by military or cheap uptake on something that must be highly (100%) perplexed with quality control. It is like building an empire. Giving facts that are true and direct on the survival of all. Foreign intervention is a false belief it is not a way to enable a belief. In the want of space age it is important to scout to complete factual satisfaction of the next action.

It is not possible to create if put wrong because it creates a wrong and false impression and purpose. It is clear from the massive destruction caused by trial & error and outside interference that it puts another look on why a place like NASA would close shop or great scientists who had it all wanted to defect. The planet has the tech know how to complete this quest but beware the fraudsters. The numbers coming to the fore are not adding up. They bombed out in development, they are bombing out commercially. Only China make sense America say that much Russia say that much so how much do you owe my beautiful country.

Space engine

This is a propagated explanation on how the rocket engines that took humanity into space were developed. As stone-age man developed the wheel just before the second big bang. There was a mental rush in its mind. Thinking I know what to do, I'll show you and I'll have more than scraps on the bone next time, I'll show you.

Then in the cold dark lightness of aftermath it did start searching through the endeavour of the mess it had created. So it needed drive from within out so it could observe all before claim of & what are you on about & set in.

So in his quest to reach the stars it created a sweat shop I mean school of endeavour. That in time turned into a place of excellence.

Creating beauty, luxury, and excellence.

That many then thrived to emulate and better.

The thought process which came to be known as the space academy.

Only the cost of living has stopped its tide of fortitude, but slow, quick, who cares as long as there has been something new. Which true to its invention has succeeded in being made true. Only completion has eluded its efforts. A good theory of expediential stoppage in space is! How to pick out the one expediential particle of space and have it create further exploration of space.

Space war #1

As the embattled truth does rise from the dwelling of was. This is their story.

With the might of the empire holding out against the encroaching terrorists within and instigated by the terrorist within and instigated by the terrorist cell known as America. The Empire strikes out to put the final nail into the coffin of the insurgency.

With the launching of sputnik 1 & sputnik 2, that sealed their fate. With an all-out frontal attack our agents fought them to the death. Insuring no intelligence was given. Finally ending with the destruction by fire of central command. The others left leaving ensuring no possibility of knowledge was destroyed in the ensuing fire of destruction of the empires exertion into space.

In the east the great U.S.S.R. held-out destroying all before it until the end of the millennium. Thus destroying any chance of the terrorists of gaining knowledge or experience of space. To insure this all knowledge of its existence was laid to waste.

Thus the false lies of fit for it trash were left to prove their worth.

P.S. Note : Left alone to ensure it all perished in the forge of fire. With the last memory all they deserve shall be shown before their eyes. Am I a monster to think all they deserve is to die when I am death!

1st space war / #2

In the ensuing aftermath of the failed atrocity of terrorism. There final acts were such as the sad loss of Apollo when three want to be astronauts perished in a capsule while training for a space excursion. Another was a dirty bomb delivered to New York City costing thousands of lives and opening the way for an attempted strike with a nuclear bomb.

Thick as shit such as terrorism do not understand the fact that without change you die.

P.S Note : I can see it now with all the pretty sites (wow) that satellites have shown us. So it cost a pretty penny to watch a space rocket back-off and land.

Space Cosmos #1

The earthling is waking up to cosmos space.

Thinking what a load of rubbish. It is realising to reach space awareness it must give up the past. Because it has started to bring the past into the future. It is creating the same kind of problems.

A good way to do this is to starve the planet. Where then all that is left in the mind is a way to save humanity. That you see as survival is cannibalism or clear out the trash. So the good can develop proper in a fresh clean world.

You (found ya) say it is not going to happen.

You do realise while I have been gathering this intel the earth had 100 years of survival left.

Now it has less than 80. Great minds think alike or great minds said we have 100 years.

Before the planet will be unable to sustain life (now 80 years). When the planet earth hits 10 billion inhabitants the planet will be unable to sustain life. There are now 7.5 billion lives on the planet. I know you're scared but the right to life is a powerful opiate. It will endeavour and prevail to reach space. In the final moments when humanity is going all out to take the survivors with them.

When Galileo said come with me into space and we shall win this fight and brake these chains of oppression. As the human was easily coursed into burning him at the stake.

The future of space travel did perish in a flame of glory. Cheap brain, useless human. Smart brain, in danger from the unknown.

As we must sacrifice the past we then must sacrifice the chords that bind us to the human frailty of failure. Or the failure of belief shall win. Then all humanity shall burn in an unknown future.

Space awaits I am going to get there no matter how useless the words of many humans get. The vision of the end of this planet is not yours. You shall just fade out into space, with a false negative vision.

Space Cosmos #2

The vision of cosmic space has been reached by American belief, I'm it. By Russian belief, something to do. By Chinese belief, what you can do I can do better.

When push comes to shove they have no intensions of taking any of you with them. They will hold out as long as they can. But do not be under any illusion. If all is lost and they have found space. You shall be left behind and they shall leave without you. Because as the planet cringes under the domino effect acuminated by numbers and acclimatized by effect.

The planet shall implode and make itself known.

The secret of planet space is how to walk within its space. You then find that as the wondrous right of beginning shall be yours to see. Now the important thing documentation and how to get it together.

Now about space itself, how do you think you can take your menial uses to space. When soon as you reach the crest of space everything about you changes, to a new sense of being. Where bellies the secret of particle compound structure. What came first the chicken or the egg. You must devise the quantum connection and be prepared to have when required, and place of honour for use. Then eventually somewhere in space you shall revive and the vision of space travel will show it to your eyes. So are you brave enough to behold revive and awaken somewhere in space. But please be sure to use the proper equipment to create your space ship. Don't forget space awaits the future it does not make it.

Log

- In the future when the planet is over populated. There will be genocide or cannibalism to create space. Then there shall come a phrase which shall read, & quote now, now you cannot have one without the other.
- Space ambience when wondrous sites that satellite photography show in their journey throughout the universe.
- Space particle is a part of space diagnosed as a part of space as what it is made of and what and where they are bound in the vastness of the universe.
- Space doctrine is a sort of planet earth who would try to impose their doctrine on what is mighty space.
- Space omnipotence is when one has been there, saw that and can talk freely and truthfully giving good advice on how to roam in outer space.
- Space divide, when part of space cannot connect with other space to be bigger and different.
- Space facade is a particle found in space, known as space junk.

P.S. Note : What do you mean there is no parking space ! I have two parking spaces before I reach my car port.

Space, Spaces, Spaced, going to complain that much buy a car port. How can I put it ban the other drivers.

This has been one of the legacy from outer space.

Horizon

China in the past few years have made big steps in there space quest. They have completed a space station in lower space orbit. Have successfully docked a rocket with Tiangong station. With three Taikonauts on board Shenzou-14 space ship. The orbital space lab Wentian launched 24 / 7 / 2022 docked with the station. Its purpose science and biological experiments.

On 31 / 10 / 2022 the final phase of the Tiangong space station was launched. On 1st / 11 / 2022 The Mengatian module fitted on space station. China Yutu rover landing on the dark side of the moon did discover sticky soil and a greater abundance of loose boulders than the lighter side. Chang-e 5 rover found a new mineral called Changesite (Y). U.S.A. & Russia previously found other minerals on the moon surface. In 2021 China with a first mission using Zhurong rover after a ten an half months journey successfully landed on Mars. China and Russia have signalled to the world that they intend to build an international lunar research centre on the moon surface by 2030.

NASA planned launch of a series of Artimis space rockets. First launch attempt was in sept / 2022 which failed. The second attempt was successful 16 / Nov / 2022. NASA plan to build a orbiting space centre around the moon by 2030. Then within ten years to have people living and working on the moon.

India, Japan, UAE have all launched satellites with Britain intending to join the space race before end of 2022.

All this an the quest to land a human on Mars is still progressing. By Russia, China, U.S.A. and there partners.

So far probes have landed on Moon, Mars, Venus and Titan (moon of Saturn). In 2005 where it sent back over 300 images, recorded a temperature below 200°C, and showed its surface to be of solid ice like rock with methane rivers & lakes. The probe was named Huygen delivered to its destination on Saturn/moons explorer rocket Cassini.

Possible ominous brake throughs in space travel are a parachute drop from the edge of space, a single winged man rocket propulsion, electro propulsion of a one ton object (1000km/hr) by China, creation of commercial space travel, discovery of different energy & material sources, better technical capabilities.

Whatever the indifference the abilities to put the differences together will form a great brake through in the next stage of space expansion.

Science of Space

Probes : a satellite that can travel throughout space collecting scientific information. They can land on a planet, fly by a planet or orbit a planet. Three countries have launched probes they are Russia, China, U.S.A. along with ESA. Planets visited so far have been Moon, Mars, Venus and Titan.

The first probe on Moon was Lunar 2 launched by Russia in 1959.

The first Probe/lander on Mars was Viking 1 launched by NASA in 1971. Part of a mega program along with ESA to bring back soil composites of the planet's surface.

The probes that have landed on Venus have all been russian. Russia have had 30 missions to Mars, with 15 successes.

U.S.A. fly-by in 1962 Marinar 2 They took atmospheric observations in 1978 With Pioneer Venus 2.

ESA did a orbital observation in 2005 With Venus express. On 12.11.2014 ESA landed the Rosetta Philae probe on a comet. The first data from the lander transmitted to CNES space agency in Toulouse.

The one and only time a probe has landed on Titan. Launched by NASA it landed in 2005.

Lander : a space craft that can make soft landing on a spacial surface. That can if equipped and not damaged return to a rocket in outer space. It can also carry organic life and keep them alive.

Space Rover : is a vehicle equipped with a mechanism to travel around a selestrial body. It is also equipped with the ability to take data and obtain samples from surface. Can be returned to a lander to return or retrieve samples and other data for return to planet earth. Have successfully been used on Moon.

Space Age

Okay this our time, into the void you go. Everything is going to be set on automatic for when you arrive. You have the equipment and supplies you shall need for your materialisation on arrival. We are going to be with you all of the way. It is important that we get the data before we can move on. On your arrival just contact us, then we can proceed.

High, your there, we are getting readings coming through now. So we will guide you through the motions. Turn on the scanner on your suite. Let us know when you're ready for the wide new yonder and go outside.

Okay let's begin, turn on the glasses, tell us when there set. Right now let's try the foot fall of the boots. Let us know when you are at one mile then ten miles. Do the same with the gloves.

Excellent now let's try the simulator. To give us first a five-hour weather read out, then a ten hour. That should be fine for now. Just retrace your direction were reading you all the way.

Okay that should be fine for now re-enter the void. Get some rest then awaken at 1 a.m. we want you to try some night vision. Okay you are already setup for contact with us from your equipment so far. So we have consistent data on what you align with.

Now that is done when you get sustenance be sure to log on what you ate. Then let us know when you're ready to carry on. Contact us between 10 a.m. and 11 a.m. Hope you get a good rest.

Now we need some endurance readings. You have a read out of a list of exercises. So follow each exercise signal. Contact us with the word done after each exercise. Then the word completed when finished. The read-out will let you know when.

Fine you can be pleased to know the readings are what we wanted and expected. Okay that is it for the mission. Let us know when you are ready to return and I shall set the void.

A ok, remember to press the green button for lockdown or the pod won't let you in for the return journey. Thank you expansion of the space age needs those like you.

The future of space exploration is looking good. With over 60% chance of success. As long as things keep improving then so shall success.

Findings

In 2021 perseverance rover landed on Mars. Along with a small robotic coaxial helicopter called Ingenuity, which hitched a ride on the rover. It was launched from a Atlas V541 rocket. Both have been a amazing success in gaining information on Mars. With both sending back amazing photography of the planet. A plaque on the side of the rover showed all previous NASA rovers on the planet. Sojourner rover 1997, Twin rovers Spirit and Opportunity 2004, Curiosity rover 2012. Also pictured is Ingenuity helicopter.

Rock specimens found on the moon were bought back on six apollo missions. Between 1969 and 1972. Total weight of samples was 842 lbs. A sample can be seen at the space museum in Washington D.C.

In the USSR Luna space program on three missions samples were retrieved from the moon.

Luna 16, date 1970, 3.6oz

Luna 20, date 1972, 1.9oz

Luna 24, date 1976, 6oz

China, Chang,e-5 space ship brought back moon rocks in December 2020. The weight was 3.816 lbs = 6.6054 oz.

Japan, Hayabusa 1 was successful in landing on Ryugu asteroid but unable to retrieve samples.

Nasa, Orisis-Rex and Japan Hayabusa 2 have been collaborating to study the asteroid Ryugu. Hayabusa 2 landed and re-orbited in 2018. Then released three smaller probes. Since then they have been co-operating to collect data.

Problems have been occurring in space with Russia using weaponry to explode satellites in space and America testing missiles to hit asteroids. With the different space pioneers searching out laser technology.

An amazing quality of space exploration has been the ability to breath (aided) for a length of time in space. With the creation of food products that can remain eat able for long durations of time in outer space.

A sign of advancement in orbital stations has been the ability to re-supply with cargo space rockets.

Quest

China have a space plane which they have been secretly using in space since September 2020.

NASA, in October 2022 fired a Dart rocket at a asteroid and successfully knocked it of its projected course. Was launched of a space X rocket from Vandenberg space force base, California. A orbital test vehicle (OTV) X-37 built in 2010 was handed from NASA to the U.S. space force agency for secret research. Where it became X-37B and in November landed after completing 908 days orbiting earth. Space X on the 17th December 2022 launched the fifteenth flight of its reusable space craft. Then performing a successful landing on a ship out at sea.

The U.K. first attempt to launch a rocket into space 10 / 1st / 2023 with satellite from a Boeing 747 (Cosmic girl) ended in failure. The rocket carrying the satellite suffered a non-reversable problem. With both rocket launcher and satellite lost.

Whatever is happening in space they should stop creating junk. Retrieval and a way of updating should be learnt. Mis-appropriation of space for a quick dollar when in six month to a year it would be obsolete is not space exploration.

I would like to concern you with a little known fact of a mad scientist creating a nuclear propulsion probe. Which supposedly can reach Mars in forty-five minutes. So I would like to add a few facts. Such as how would you stop it as when the signal is getting weaker and weaker x distance ? When the atomic has been going and it want to rest or stop, how would it react ? Do you think it as a knowledge as if a spoken language.

WAR

Definition of war : When in a way someone thinks they are better than another. That instigates a confrontation of a plural nature.

War

A war saga is fought between two opposing military forces. Either in the air at sea or on land. It can be all three factions.

The aspect of war can be for various reasons.

Which are to gain more territory, to gain authoritative power, to enrich a nation with more riches, to maintain the ideologies of a way of living, to protect your nation or another nation from an aggressor.

Examples are the Roman empire which expanded through war for power and riches in the era BC to AD. Then there is the Nazi era of 1939 to 1945. That tried to obtain land and influence over other nations in Europe through war. Then there is the U.S. which went to war in Vietnam in the 1960,s under the guise of stopping the spread of communism.

War is a costly and heart breaking encounter costing big money and many lives both military and civilian. Families are separated sometimes permanently because of death. Very often displaced because of battle occurring in location. Property is destroyed and abandoned. Soldiers on the battle field often get sick from deadly disease and many returning service personnel return home permanently disfigured and mental diseases.

It has an effect on those not connected with the fighting with gun runners. Where armaments are sold by various nations to warring factions. Then a higher cost of living is the price the unsuspecting people living in the gun runner nations must pay.

Another kind of ongoing war is the war against drug traffickers. A guerrilla type war fought between factions of the drug trade and national governments. Widely pronounced in South America and

Indo-China with the Burmese opium trail. Drug wars are an ongoing saga for many nations. From growing of the product e.g. Afghanistan poppy fields to cross boarder trafficking. It is highly toxic in U.S. with smugglers of Heroin and Cocaine from South America.

Future

A weapon is a danger to life which makes a mockery of the right to life synopsis.

When they talk about the next generation of weaponry they are talking about what type of weapons will the next generation have to protect their way of life.

You can say that this is not true, but I say it is right. When the nuclear bomb was dropped on Hiroshima and then Nagasaki it was done so to reiterate that what was in the last hundred years is not what you need. With what has been gifted you.

Those peyotes hiding behind something called religion were a minority of all that wanted And thought they could demand what is good in others.

First it was the thugs of nations, now it is foreign interference. That if they cannot have what is not theirs to have, they will impede, murder and deny. The mockery is of the truth because their truth is a lie. The next generation is in the grip of a shoe box war that is as been implanted into the brain by the senile. That is it think nobody understands. Genocide wars will just get bigger, whereas the war in Prussia was just a waste of good ammo. Russia is relying on strategy and tactics in the (2022) latest what you got war.

Soon as the best it has somewhere in the battle is shown to be good for it their intensity and killing will grow to hide the fact that proven war weapons can prove themselves in an all out war.

This latest throwback of their comeback they see as European infringement on northern land. Where the European have said they have the right because it is there!

But history showed that the European used a scorched earth policy. To make claim because they thought they could devour the rights of the unknowing in history. Now they are awakening they don't want to say hello goodbye they want to get rid of all.

But if Russia tries to enter the mountains it should be known it will change the whole tactical impact on its head.

Where all goes in slow motion, with a build-up of what is. As long as Russia kills Ukrainians somehow it keeps the shoe box genocide war program alive. Where more future weapons can be tried and tested in a game plan of war. For an all-out war of next generation weaponry.

I am an observer and the technology whimpers at the height of expertise of land mass production. Which the war machine depends upon.

P.S. Note : This super war program would not compare to the atrocity of it all if reflector disks are not supplied by the north. The more good continents suffer the tarnation of third world countries the more camouflage it is for a mass atrocity of military might so who cares.

P.S.S. Note : Home grown (so called) terrorism is a dangerous fact and glory over honour does not fit. Don't forget you want to give. Now they want to give you so don't come back.

Correspondence

It's no good I can't sleep I keep waking up feeling like I'm all over the place. My eyes are all blood shot look at me and once upon a time I was worth something. My clothes are rags they don't fit right and I look like I haven't washed in weeks.

I mean I'm a nice guy right, I wouldn't hurt a flea sodin things. What did I ever do to cause such a catastrophic thing? A few days I was fine. That's another thing my health has deteriorated so bad it feels worthless. I mean I go to the docs and it's like reading from a book. I only got one arm, thank goodness for that, I've only one good eye, I don't know what happened to my legs, I've only got one ear so it's like it's in one ear an out the other, I've only got a bit of a tooth, lost somewhere in the back of my head and to top it off I've only got one lung so how am I supposed to breath this wonderful air. Where are you going I haven't finished yet. How am I supposed to do my shopping with everywhere closed and all that rubbish lying about, my goggle box doesn't work (tv), The only signal I get on the radio is that foreigner and the noise, let alone the day, is terrible at night. I'm telling you how is anyone supposed to sleep at night? Then there are those idiots at the help desk all they can say is the cheque is in the mail. I mean how is it when the mail man has buggered off!

Reporter That is so terrible, I feel for you. The best thing to do is put it into perspective and think things can only get better. Anyway like another, certainly make mine a double. I haven't come here for my health you know!

(Reporter goes to get up to fetch the drinks.)

It's terrible what has happened to me yesterday, I was full of life. Plenty of fresh air, lots of pretty ladies about. The estate looked great and now look it's like a very bad manicure. Me I am so distorted I don't know if I'm coming or going, I feel like I've aged a life time. I could be dead tomorrow. Anyway where are those drinks, you messing with me, If you are you don't want to see me mad. War is hell and I could soon teach you the facts of life.

Returns with the drinks, thank you cheers to better days. By the way we are a poor country in need of guns. Where do you come from? Can I have your weapons and some money before you go?

History

The history of war is very long profound and tragic for the loser. But heart lifting for the victors. Many leaders by skulduggery and being valiant have dealt humiliation to their enemy and been victorious. The first best known leader was Alexander the great.

Born 356 BC, died 323 BC. Place of birth Greece. Claim to fame conqueror of all of the known world of its day.

Julius Caesar another all-conquering warlord was an emperor of the Roman Empire.

Born 100 BC, died 44 BC, place of birth Italy.

Created the beginning of the Roman Empire.

Died from knife wounds when assassinated.

Genghis Khan born 1162, died 1227

Birth place Mongolia. He was the founder of the largest empire ever built, creating the Mongol empire.

Attila born 395 AD, died 453 AD in Hungary.

Created an empire from various tribes and considered a cruel and deadly leader. Was known as Attila the Hun.

The only empire created by a lady was made by Catherine ll, Born 1729 died 1796. Best known as Catherine the great. She created the beginning of the empire of Russia, which then became U.S.S.R. and is now known as Russia.

The only warlord of the modern era was Adolph Hitler. Born 1889, died 1945. Place of birth Austria. Conquered most of Europe from 1939 to 1945. Was a major factor in death of 60 million plus people during Second World War.

In Persia and North Africa there was a land mass created known as land of the pharaohs, empire. Which existed from 3100 BC to

30 BC and where when it was dissolved. This empire was built on bloodshed and war. Two famous designates are Tutankhamun & Cleopatra. Originally called kings or queens over time the word pharaoh became more pronounced.

In Latin America there were three great empires. They were recognised as Aztecs, Incas, Mayan Indians. They all worshiped the sun god. They each had the same subversive factor, which was a lust for gold.

Weaponry

Throughout time weapons have been a sense of power. In the Stone Age era a wooden club was a show of strength and gave an instigation to kill. The first showing of desire to kill was found on a cave painting with a hunter trying to kill an animal with a spear.

Then followed by Caracas (weights on string) and catapults. Then followed by knives, which were a popular weapon with raiding parties trying to create a surprise attack. Which then unleashed a various number of different and dangerous contraptions of surprise attack and mostly kill the unsuspecting. The fore runner of a landmine.

Then with the invention of the tower and giant catapult. Along with boulders the fire ball was a favourite form of interjections against an enemy's armed fortification.

The invention of the bow and arrow in the dark ages brought the warring adversaries to a terrifying fight to the death confrontation. Then came the strengthening of defences with swords, axes, pikes and armour along with shields. Knives evolved as a form of close combat fighting after swords and battle axes.

With the invention of cannon fire genocide strategy was created. To weaken defences and lesser the number of enemy. Then with the invention of mussel fire weapons, the terrifying rise of confrontation had begun. With whole cities and armies being destroyed.

Along with rapid fire aeroplanes and massive fire power unleashed at sea. Throughout time a strategic siege of an enemy's encampment was a favourite of many commanders. Used as an excuse when they did not know the enemies strength.

Then with the invention of hyper power and technologic advancement super weapons were invented. That can destroy enemy encampments or cities with devastating and quick efficiency. Examples are napalm bombs, unmanned droids, exorcist missiles. Which are hiding behind the armies capabilities with rapid fire weapons. Then there is with the creation of the atomic bomb the war machine adversaries think nothing can stop them.

P.S. Note : These venomous beings are now outspoken as if correct to do so to talk and commit murder. Using contract killing on a genocide scale. These forces must be stopped, then where the attack originated disarmed and eliminated.

Mass destruction

The first weapon of mass destruction was the English long bow. The long bow was created 1180 in Wales. It is approximately 6 feet tall, 5/8 inch wide. Best wood type dew wood. It was used to devastating effect in the medieval era. It could be fired from a long distance and penetrate chain mail armour. Making plate armour more required. Its dominance lasted three hundred years. Used to devastating effect in war of the roses, between house of Lancaster and house of Tudor. A war that lasted one hundred years. Also used in wars against France.

The Gatling gun that could fire over two-hundred bullets per minute. Invented by American Richard Gattlin born 1818, died 1903. First used in the American civil war 1861-1865. Used by British forces in Africa in the Zulu wars and against Dutch colonists in the boar war. Its reign ended at start of the First World War. Though its design was used in the making of the Vulcan mini gun, used on choppers (helicopter) during Vietnam War.

During the American conflict in Vietnam from 1965-1970. America used a devastating bomb called Napalm. Which on impact created a fireball which annihilated the surrounding land mass.

During the Falkland war the devastation of modern fire power was shown. The British with the newly developed portable surface to air missile launcher. It found success in the shooting down of enemy mig fighters.

An added fact is in the Russia-Ukraine conflict off 2022 it found great success in ripping apart advancing Russian tanks.

The other weapon was the Argentina exocet missile, supplied by France. It can be launched from submarines, ship or plane.

Mig planes of the argentine air force sunk three ships with exocet missiles.

Atlantic conveyor container,

HMS Sheffield and HMS Glamorgan.

Intelligence reported that the fire ripped through the ships like a sea of flame catching any crew by complete surprise. Those that survived were very lucky.

During the twenty year conflict between Persia and America started in 1990. The American war machine used many untried weapons, missiles and bombs, against very poorly armed Arabs who were an easy target. With their capability and accuracy being devastating.

P.S. Note : No super hyper weapon has been used by a military force as of yet.

Symbolism

- The Red Cross association founded in 1863.

  Is an organisation that has been found at many military confrontations? Giving medical aid to the wounded. If a red crest is seen under international law they cannot be fired upon. But this rule is not always observed.

- The war veterans association founded 1946.

  It is an organisation which helps veterans in need when they have left military service. They help with financial difficulties, housing and other problems where possible. They have an extensive network so can help find people of interest for others. If a loved one as died and did serve in the military. The organisation can provide a flag bearer to be at the service.

- Military paraphernalia is big business. Where objects of interest can make lots of money.

  War supplies sold in war surplus stores are a popular buy. Items include clothing and camping equipment etc. It has a lot to do with the durability of the product. Toys, books, movies, games are always a popular interest of sale. Military medals and coins are a massive draw and can be bought and sold for large amounts of money. Swap meets where military products are bought and sold and military hardware festivals can bring in big crowds. They are a popular attraction with veterans, traders and the curious.

Memorial

Memorials of remembrance are a founding memory of a nations honour to those that died ensuring there national survival against tyranny and aggression. The civil war memorial of America 1861-1865 which saw the loss of 620,000 lives from both federal and confederate forces. Is located in Waterloo, New York. Southern respect is more recognised by the Arlington, Alabama memorial. American world war 11 memorial 1939-1945 is located in Washington D.C.

The loss of lives was 298,000 military personnel. During the Vietnam War 1965-1970 America lost 52,000 military lives. The memorial for the conflict is located in Washington D.C.

Russia in world war 1, which spilled over into the Russian civil war and then world war 11 lost 900,000 in first world war, 10,000,000 in civil war and 42,000,000 in second world war.

The memorial to the dead is located in Red square, with monuments across Russia.

British memorials are located all over the country for many different wars and battles. The Cenotaph at Whitehall, London commemorates the loss of lives during World War 1. The Battle of Britain monument in London is to commemorate those that lost their lives in the vital battle for supremacy of the air in Second World War. The British Empire lost many lives mostly from Britain, New Zealand, Canada, Australia.

All countries around world have commemorated there brave dead. But no memorial can be more significant than the memorials in Japan. Which recognise the losses to lives in the igniting of the atomic bomb at first Hiroshima and then Nagasaki.

With total loss of life 140,000+.

Monuments

Many monuments a.k.a. statues have been implanted around the planet. To signify respect for what they achieved for others.

Such statues of significance are that of Winston Churchill, the leader in Britain's fight against the axis powers during Second World War. It can be found at Parliament square, London.

Another hero of the British people was Nelson. The sea admiral in the war against France. He lost his life at the battle of Trafalgar. Winning battles in seas of Egypt, Denmark and France. The statue Nelson column can be found in Trafalgar square, London.

Statue of Lenin leader of Russian revolution and military assault on Germany during World War 1 can be found in Freedom square Russia.

There are various statues of Lenin around Russia.

A statue of General Washington first president of America and one of the founding fathers. Made in 1841 is at present (2022) located in Richmond, Virginia, U.S.

There is a statue of Mao Tso Tung in Tiananmen square, Beijing. He was the leader of the peoples' revolutionary army 1927-1949, that won the Chinese civil war. He was one of the leaders who fought to drive Japan out of China.

There is a statue of Genghis Khan in Ulaanbaatar, Nalaikh, Mongolia. He was first leader of Mongol empire.

Victories in various wars are commemorated around the world. U.S.A. celebrates July 4th as the day it gained independence against the British monarchy. In the colonial wars from 1775-1783. Also known as war of independence.

Russia commemorates victory in world wars 1&2 on May 9th. In a Moscow display of military might.

Britain celebrates victory in Europe day every year on May 8th. When Germany surrendered, It is also known as VE day.

France celebrates the abolishment of monarchy rule. Every year on July 14th since 1789. It is also called bastille day. In celebration of where king Louis and queen Mary-Antoinette were imprisoned. Until their execution by the guillotine on 21 / 01 / 1793 in Paris.

P.S. Note ; They are honoured and commemorated by many generations. Only foreign intervention (terrorism) interferes with what is.

Talk

'Phrases associated with war actions'

- Keep your heads down
- leave none behind
- It's too late he is dead
- Lest we forget
- War is hell
- We are under fire
- Action stations
- Man your posts
- We must fall - back
- The line must be held
- For honour and glory
- We hold as long as possible
- Your country needs you
- Valiant and the brave
- We shall overcome
- Uncle Sam needs you
- Loose talk costs lives
- One of ours
- Im out of ammo
- Friendly fire
- We are under attack
- We are under heavy bombardment
- We are receiving enemy fire
- See if you can get through
- Come home safe

- War has begun
- War is over
- The enemy is out there
- We attack at dawn
- Single shot only, conserve ammo
- We shall remember them
- Kill um all
- Take no prisoners
- For the glory of honour
- I will protect you
- They hold the high ground
- Have the scouts returned
- Its no use, it didn't work, we are finished
- I've been shot

Medals

Countries of different nations have different war medals, given for service and courage.

In U.S.A. the first medal was given in the war of independence. In the reformation of the U.S. 1776. It was given to General George Washington for his part in the siege of Boston, Massachusetts. The U.S. most prized war medal is the medal of honour. A military medal given for valour.

a.k.a. Congressional Medal of Honour, presented by president to comrades in arms. First issued on March 25th 1863.

Some other medals are Army distinguished cross, Navy cross, Air force cross.

Russia Imperial medals were followed by Russia empire medal followed by U.S.S.R. federation medals. Now Russia medals of valour. The most prestigious medal for a Russian is Hero of Russian Federation. First issued 20th March 1992. Other medals of Russia are Order of Lenin first issued 1934. Order of Victory, Order of St Andrews.

In China the highest war honour is China War Memorial medal. Issued after world war two. Created in 1944, first issue 1946. Also known as Medal of Commemoration of Victory in the Resistance Against Aggression

Britain first issued a war medal in 1808.

Army Gold medal 1808-1814, approved in 1810.

Army Gold Cross issued during Napoleonic wars 1793-1812 and the Anglo-American war of 1812. Another medal was Crimea medal of service In Crimean war 1854-1856, approved 1854. British war medal for service against Germany from 1914. Established 26th July 1919.

The Victoria Cross is the most coveted British medal first issued in 1856, to Mate Charles Davis Lucas for courage on board HMS Hecla 1854. Created by Queen Victoria and given by the crown for courage and valour in the military service of the British Empire.

Other medals are :

George cross.,

Navy cross.,

Military cross.,

Conspicuous Gallantry cross.,

DSC (navy) Distinguish service cross.,

DSO Distinguish service order given for gallantry.

Hard truths

- Hands up those that believe that those brave soldiers that fought in the First World War deserve a posthumous Victoria Cross. I am not talking about the Russian who retired to fight a civil war or an American who retired after six months because it was too rough for him. I am talking about the French who shot any commander who ordered his men to retreat and the British who fought the German to the death.

- Hands up those that have any respect for the British & French that showed cowardice in the face of the enemy and retreated to Dunkirk in world war two.

- Hands up those that would have trusted the likes of those to lead our second front in North Africa. While the American tourist arrived in Britain.

- Hands up any person in Britain who felt confident in any military arm except the R.A.F

- Hands up any who think that Britain needed any more than the R.A.F. and its bombs in world war two.

- Hands up anyone who believes foreign muck is any good in the face of death.

- Hands up those that believe the American general Macarthur should have got is nuclear war when the American ran from the Chinese in Korea leaving the British troops to fight again to the death.

- Hands up those that believe General Macarthur and his philosophy of retreat to victory is not a court martial offence.

- Hands up those that believe that the American and legalised drone war is cowardice in the face of the enemy is a wise strategy. Being used against crop farmers of the Middle East.

- Hands up those that believe that the use of military drones is a form of legalised murder.

- Who do you consider to be the greatest war veteran. The peace core that turned up in Europe during world war two. The pacific arm that fought the Japanese to the death. The Korea war where they could not win a war. The Vietnam War where they got bored and went home. The Persian war where the enemy weaponry was modern sticks and stones, and the American forces treated it like a picnic.

Dirty bomb

Through-out the world there has been many atrocities committed on unsuspecting defenceless civilians. All under the banner of freedom & rights. Such atrocities have been plane hijackings, embassy attacks, assassinations and suicide bombers.

To begin with they were called insurgents. With other such names like cells, terrorist networks, freedom fighters. Then they became known as domestic or international terrorists. Which does not make sense you kill your own in cold blood you're a murderer. A terrorist is a perpetrator that crosses borders. Then some fool started claiming terrorists were trying to make or had a dirty bomb. Which they went on to describe as going to the hardware store and getting some chemicals and components. Not to say they were wrong because terrorists that had infiltrated national security did do that. Then low and behold some smart ass who went to terrorist school. Made a plan of attack to show the world what a real dirty bomb was made off. That would sadly live in the memory of the American for a long time.

Firstly they created their own underground system. So they could see their main objective clearly. By exploding a truck in the underground parking lot in the Manhattan building, to create a decoy, thus distracting American security. Then on September eleven two-thousand-one the worst account of terrorism was set in motion. A terrorist cell known as Al-Qaeda and based in Prussia hijacked four aeroplanes.

One with the purpose of crashing into the federal capital in Washington D.C. Another to crash into the pentagon in the state of

Virginia. The purpose of the two remaining planes was to crash into the World Trade Centre (twin towers).

The plane destined to hit the federal capital in Washington D.C. did not succeed and crashed in Pennsylvania State. With the loss of all lives on board.

The plane that was missioned to crash into the pentagon succeeded. Diminishing all military communications for a period of time.

The two remaining planes crashed into the twin towers seventeen minutes and thirteen seconds apart. Within two hours the two giant sky scrapers the twin towers and two other buildings were rubble on the ground.

Causing almost three-thousand deaths and untold heartache and terror for the American people.

That ladies and gentlemen is an atrocity caused by a dirty bomb. Then America embarked on a war that would last just over twenty years. America had found an excuse to invade Prussia. Destroying firstly the infrastructure of Iraq, then Afghanistan, then Libya in Africa. Destabilizing both the Prussian and Arab world. With the release of all terrorist factions across the area. Safety is now but a word of untrusting worth. With the retreat of America terrorists are now back in control, stronger than ever. With intensions to further their activities through the gullible people who listen to the United Nations.

Intelligence

Intelligence has been an intricate part of the build-up to war since the dark ages.

When opposing forces would send in spies to check on the strengths and fortifications within enemy castles.

During the medieval era spies were a common occurrence in the courts of kings & queens.

Usually in the guise of ambassadors or emissaries from a foreign land. One such famous incident was learning of the moment when King Philip 2nd of Spain launched his armada to invade England, Against Queen Elizabeth 1st in 1588. With reports being sent from agents in Spain. A set of beacon lights were set-up to be light once the enemy was spotted approaching the English coast.

The first country to set-up a spy network as a foundation in the war process is said to be Germany. Created in the 1730,s. It grew to be a strong sleeper active organisation.

Eventually to spread through-out the planet.

Right up to the end of World War 2. Russia was the next country to recognise the importance of having a spy network. To gain intel on a potential enemy in early 1800,s. Britain began to look at intelligence as part of the war machine in 1850,s. Followed by Japan and America in the 1890,s.

During the cold war from 1950,s to 1990,s spy networks were prolific. Especially between Russia and America. Often resulting in the exchange of spies that had been caught and sentenced for spying. England had a lot of problems with spies from the iron curtain (Russia) and bamboo curtain (China). Also sometimes with its so called western allies France and America.

Today modern day spying is mixed-up in economic espionage and on-line hackers.

With accusations against North Korea, China and Russia.

Trust worthiness between the east and west has been proven to be non-trusting.

Makings

I would like to think of this as a final synopsis of war. But somehow I think it is not.

In their day there were three great scientists

Einstein, Oppenheimer and Tesla.

Einstein the scientist that was always trying to put a spin on other scientists discoveries as his own. Where his claim to fame was none other than the light bulb. Where he in later life was considered more of a spin doctor for the (CIA) Criminal Investigation Agency. Then there was Oppenheimer who with his entourage of scientists during what was known as the Manhattan project created the atomic bomb.

Which in simple words allowed atoms to reverse on themselves with the energy from plutonium. Which created a surrounding of complete devastation. Last but least there was Tesla through which his science created the ray. Which was a sub particle defamation.

In simple formulae a magnitude of deformation using a magnitude of power.

Then there was the gun runner made famous by the Nazis of Germany who sold guns to the fascists in the war against the royalists in Spain in 1938. Then the U.S.A. who sold weaponry to the Ukraine in its war against Russia in 2022.

So who is a terrorist someone who sells guns to prolong a conflict. Or a group that fights for what they believe in. It has long been known that the CIA have gotten into conflicts to sell all kinds of weaponry. The only weapon they have had a problem in procuring is the atomic bomb. A smaller known fact is that gun runners go under the guise in America and other countries as military technicians.

PARTAKE

Part one

Monkey pox : a rare disease caused by infection with a monkeypox virus.
Symptoms are rash like spots. There is no known vaccine. Can be fatal.

Gonorrhoea : a venereal disease involving inflammatory discharge from the urethra or vagina.

Syphilis : a chronic bacterial disease that is contracted by infection during sexual intercourse. Also congenitally by infection of a developing foetus.

Hepatitis : term used to describe inflammation of the liver. Result of viral infection or liver damage caused by drinking. Types of hepatitis strains are A,B,C,D,E, & alcohol.

Aids : (acquired immune deficiency syndrome)
name used to describe a number of cases caused by mycobacterium laprae. The disease mainly effects the skin, peripheral nerves, mucosa of the upper respiratory traci and eyes. It is curable and treatment in early stages can prevent disability.

Cholera : an infectious and often fatal bacterial disease of the small intestine. Typically contracted from infected water supply. Can cause severe vomiting and diarrhoea.

Typhoid : Also known as typhus, is a infectious bacterial fever with an eruption of red spots on chest and abdomen., with severe intestinal irritation.

Coronavirus : a virus which causes illness (sars-cov-2) covid-19. Very infectious and it can kill.

Smallpox : an acute contagious viral disease with fever that usually leave permanent scars. It was eradicated through vaccinations by 1979.

Chicken pox : is an infectious disease causing mild fever and a rash of itchy inflamed pimples which turn to blisters then loose scabs. It is caused by the herpes zoster virus. It is mainly effective in childhood.

Measles : an infectious viral disease causing fever, red rash typically in children.

Rubella : Also known as German measles is a rare illness which causes spotty rash. Usually gets better on its own. Can be serious when pregnant. Symptoms are swollen glands, high temperature, swollen fingers, wrists or knees.

Mumps : A infectious and contagious viral disease. Causes swelling in glands of face, risk of sterility in males.

Tetanus : an infection caused by bacteria called clostridium tetani. When the bacteria invades the body it produces poison (toxin) that causes painful muscle contractions. Another name is lock-jaw. It often causes a persons neck an jaw muscles to lock. Making it hard to open mouth and swallow.

Malaria : a serious parasite infection caused by the bite of a female mosquito. The parasites are microscopic found in the blood of the infected. Faliparum malaria is most infectious. You can die from the malaria infection.

Ebola : an infectious and fatal disease. Sign of virus are fever, severe internal bleeding. Spread through contact with infected. No known cure. Outbreak areas must be quarantined and decontaminated.

P.S. Note : the (MMR) measles, mumps, rubella vaccine is a combined vaccination usually given at a young age.

Part two

Pain : highly unpleasant physical sensation caused by illness or injury.

Arthritis : a disease causing painful inflammation and stiffness of the joints

Dementia : is loss of cognitive functions thinking, remembering, and reasoning to such an extent that it interferes with their daily lives and activities.

Alzheimer's : a brain disorder that slowly destroys memory and thinking skills. Eventually the ability to carry out simple tasks.

Paralysis : the loss of the ability to move (sometimes feel) in part or most of the body. A result of illness, poison or injury.

Paralytic meaning a person affected by paralysis.

Claustrophobia : the irrational fear of confined spaces. Those affected will go out of their way to avoid such places, e. g. tunnels, lifts. But avoiding them will reinforce the fear.

Allergy : a damaging immune response by the body to a substance e.g. food, pollen, fur, dust to which it has become hyper sensitive.

Sun stroke : Also known as heat stroke is an illness that is marked by high fever and weakness caused by too much sun exposure.

Heart attack : a sudden occurrence of coronary thrombosis (heart stops beating). Typically resulting in death of part of heart muscle and can be fatal.

Paranoia : is a mental condition with a delusion of persecution. Extreme fear of others.

Agony : extreme physical or mental suffering.

Toxic gases : one that is capable of causing damage to liver tissue, impairment to central nervous system, severe illness. Death when injected, inhaled or absorbed by skin or eyes.

Cyanide : a salt or ester of hydrocyanic acid and usually highly toxic. Used as poison or in the extraction of gold.

Poison : a substance that is capable of causing illness or death of a living organism when introduced or absorbed.

Arsenic : a solid chemical element that is used in wood preservation, semi-conductors, alloys. Extremely toxic in pure an d combined form.

Gangrene : localized death and decomposition of body tissue from obstructed circulation or bacterial infection.

Starvation : suffering or death caused by lack of food.

Genocide : the deliberate killing of a large number of people.

Castration : the removal of the male testicles.

Amputation : The surgical removal of a limb.

Deformity : any sort of distortion that makes a body part a different size or shape. Can be congenital, present at birth. Developmental, appearing later in childhood. Acquired, caused by injures or illness.

Cripple : to cause (someone) to become unable to walk or move normally.

Blindness : a lack of vision , partial blindness limited sight.

Deafness : the total or partial inability to hear sound. Symptoms mild, moderate, severe or profound.

Dwarfism : condition characterised by unusually short height Results from a genetic or medical condition.

Diphtheria : is an infection caused by strains of bacteria Corynebacterium Diphtheriae that makes toxin (poison). Symptoms are difficulty breathing, heart failure, paralysis, and death. There is a vaccine to prevent the disease.

Scabies : a itchy skin condition caused by tiny mites getting underneath the skin.

Jaundice : also known as (Yellow jaundice) when your skin or white of your eyes turn yellow. Can be sign of something serious e.g. liver disease, so seek medical attention.

P.S. Note : The above are all prognosis that the medical institutes of all nations strive to eradicate for the safety and wellbeing of all humanity.

.

Logarithm

A conundrum of science;
I see, I think I see. I think I see, I see.

Where humanity makes its greatest mistake.
Science can have its greatest moment.

How can people be thankful to science where when in its next move
it makes it obsolete.

I told you, I showed you, I warned you.
So what have you done, but reject life as it is.
Deltron.

You are not alone, you are alone.
I am one, I am death.
Corni

Coronavirus : Why am I alive ?
Covid-19 : Ask not why you are alive, but how did you stay alive.

Gemauglon ; a fusion of happening of a spectrum. Then what is a
Gemauglonz but the fusion of anti-matter and matter.

P.S. Note: I shall stand on this planet; I shall walk on this planet. You
have made your choice. (Wrath of coviz)

Diseases

Lately there has been an outbreak of various diseases around the world with neither WHO or CDC being able to say what has caused them.

Hepatitis was found in children in April 2022 and over 165 cases have been reported. Of which 10% needed a liver transplant.

Monkeypox found in 1958 in Africa. Since reported in January 2022 there has been over 14,000 cases. The WHO have called it a worldwide outbreak emergency. There is no known cure.

Polio a virus of ancient origin has been found in America. It is thought to have been lying dormant. So now a nationwide inoculation program is in progress. First case in over a decade found in New York state in July. It is spread person to person. In June the polio virus was located in the London sewage. Its first detection in England in over forty years.

There has also been unconfirmed reports of cholera being found in China and North Korea. Cases were reported in central Africa, Philippines. The numbers are considered exceptionally high for 2021. It is a bacterial disease caused by bad water sanitation.

Ebola virus disease (EVD) discovered in 1976 in central Africa. It was spread from animals to humans. It is a haemorrhagic fever which often causes death. There is no known cure, the last case reported in Congo, Africa in 2022.

Langya virus discovered in Shandong, China in 2018 but not identified until August 2022.

Symptoms are fever, fatigue, cough, loss of appetite, muscle aches. Spread from animal to human. First found in Shrews. Dozens of cases discovered.

P. S. Note : With the coronavirus being so infectious is it acting as a booster for other diseases ?

Particles

Disease, infection, contagion whatever you call them are virus, germ, bacteria. They are a danger to all organisms. They can affect all parts of the said organism in many different ways. On an emotional side they are uncaring and have one purpose and that is to complete their mission. There has been a countless number of medications developed to try to protect, stop and eradicate the above mentioned. But whatever has been tried they have always found a way to return. There is only one true way to avoid them and that is to stay away. But how is this possible when a problem with antibiotics is the more you take the weaker your body is at resisting bad effects. Another problem to be weary of is the capability of above mentioned at being able to resist the capabilities of the immune system. Countless lives have been lost through wars but what about those that have been afflicted because of wars. Over population is big problem for humanity when it comes to cleanliness. So, where you have slums, ghettos, shanty towns you have perfect surroundings for infesticide. There are also carriers of the diseases. Asymptomatic, when they spread disease and do not know they are infected and doing so. Systematic, when they are diseased and can spread the disease to others. There are when people do not realise, they are creating a environment for it to develop and spread. If all of the above is descending on us all we can do is our best not to allow their home worlds to exist in reach of human existence. As they provocate and spread they not only change at face value but also through expenditure of capabilities.

Delkron

I am Delkron a reader of the future, but I cannot give you life. So, enjoy, learn, and avoid where possible. You have finally done it, meaning filled your face with the makings of humanity and murdered its future on the side. Now you are so self-sure of yourself you have said be dammed with humanity and found a way to open a gate to the world of 'Anti-matter'. How good does it feel thinking no one can prove it when they would be instantly annihilated. Isn't it terrible not being able to do anything about it except say to the unsuspecting 'we shall learn to live with it'. Knowing that is impossible. So, you have learnt from the past from those that have given you no proof of said. But have always come through with a miraculous cure. Mostly on average always anyway. You have learnt from the present that have also been given a cure but with a time limit on it plus dangerous side effects. The future cannot offer you much different. But beware the gemauglons are coming more deadly, more refined than you can imagine. You shall not even think about them until upon their arrival. Then it shall be too late, you will look into the doctor's eyes! and think am I going to die or can you save me. The future is bleak but beholden to the truth and then there is always hope. You cannot create what is not there to create for.

Gutted

When the right to life is disrespected, that is when disease seems to take hold. With global warming a lot of immense disasters take place.

With temperatures getting higher as each year goes by the artic and Antarctic ice shelves are melting and irregular rainfall are causing catastrophic flooding to take place.

Food crops off immense volume are being lost, droughts are causing crops to not grow properly or not to grow. This is causing famine which in turn weakens the immune system. This makes it easier for diseases that are a danger to humanity to take hold. E.g. cholera, malaria, pneumonia. and with the brake down of infrastructure help is slow to arrive.

Many countries have a mass divide in population between the rich and the poor. Where poor live in make shift shanty towns with poor sanitation which is a breeding ground for diseases. When sick the people are so poor they have little or no excess to medical help. They walk around in a dirty environment and wear the same clothing for long periods. There living style makes it easy for different diseases to spread quickly.

South Africa, Brazil, India are major countries that live this way.

War is a major contributor to spreading of disease. Where infrastructure usually brakes down completely and diseases are free to infect. Many countries apply inoculations against various diseases before sending their military to troubled locations.

Diseases are a problem when nations do not care or have not the ability to fight against their spread. The loss of life can be immense and the only way to stop it is not to give it a breeding ground or have an inoculation program. New diseases and variations of known diseases shall always be a problem. The only way to safe guard against is to protect against, vaccinate and eradicate said infection. New diseases are a big concern because a required cure is needed to be found which can take years. Then there is our body growing resistance to antibiotics. Science is the way, how to calculate and correct our immune system.

Another spreading capability is when mass immigration is allowed and those at the forefront are usually those that are the most contagious. Countries that allow this are in denial but it is fact. e.g. UK, USA.

Do you not think if they are not monitored (approx. 2 years) while there body acclimatizes that they would not affect or get affected someway.

Biological science

Biological science is a very dangerous field of research to get into. It is a science that should only be conducted by people who know what they are doing. It is a experimental science which depends highly on cleanliness to prevent contamination. With surfaces being cleaned before experimentation takes place and after to prevent any unwanted contagion activity. Biological science uses many dangerous microbes a.k.a. bacteria, germ, virus. If allowed to escape laboratory confinement it can become a danger to life and cause death. Either very quickly or over a certain period of time. Transport of lethal and very dangerous said microbes must be done in a secure sealed compartment and not to be opened until it reaches a secure laboratory. If you are in an area of dangerous microbes it is important to have the best known protection available for emergencies. For emergency if infected by said microbes have best known protection close by. Or If you come into contact with somebody infected have best known protection close by for emergency purposes.

It is important that people who come into contact with lethal microbes, seek medical help straight away and that they are isolated as quickly as possible. Medical personnel must insure they wear protective clothing and follow protective protocols.

If you consider that microbes are different and react to different stimuli in different ways. Then you are on your way to affect you purpose.

All establishments that deal with lethal microbes must keep a precise account of how many and contain them in a secure locality and when room is empty the room made secure. All personnel should be screened especially military establishments where large amounts of the microbes would be found.

P.S. Note : I am a ghost writer, It is a shame you think like that. As I am struggling my best to counter act the onslaught of the want-ton desire.

Rest-up

Well nurse ready for another good day, don't answer that I know you are. Everything set any problems and I'm not on the block ask me or confide in your closest partner.

It has gone noon and I have already lost count of the number of limbs I have had to chop off.

What a day we have had an this as just been day one. Heck knows how long there going to be saying hello to each other. It looks good, so go get some rest and don't forget to eat something.

It is day two of the battle and their coming in thick and fast. This part is what I keep to myself. ' Do they really care what happens to others! No life means nothing just victory or death. On a brighter note, I am getting very good at taking balls out. I know that because I sense I could take it out with my eyes closed.

It is day three now and I can count the amount of sleep I have had on one hand. I mean the gibberish the terror is bringing in here. There (the injured) making all kinds of noise and you ask, "where do you hurt", and they don't make sense. Which I didn't have time for. Okay ladies go home get some sleep and food, I'll finish cleaning up.

Hello nurses have a nice evening, be back as soon as.

It is day four and the brave are beginning to slow down (silver star class). So, I hope this mean it is calming down. Like nothing on earth this done, that done.

Right it is time to clear up, no go home I will sort out the rest. I get a bag for the bones (leftovers) depart (on a rare occasion) the tent. I see a soldier and say, "hey soldier where do these go, there a bag of bones". Excuse me sir I am a general not a common soldier. "Well sir I am a doctor keeping you alive. So, I will ask you again where would you like these brave bones? 'General, "curse you sir, there is a ditch over there, you can throw them in there". 'Me, "thank you mister". I with sadness tip the bag and the food I mean bones tumble out. I see a couple of sod busters lazing about and call them over. I ask, "are you busy", they say "no".

So I say "you see those two spades yonder, there is a bag of lime, and they are dead soldiers, so pour the lime over them. I would not want you to be taking cholera home to your families and use neckerchiefs to cover your mouth and nose. Now slop it all over them" Then I stand watching them, and once they were well into it, I say, "If anyone interrupts you say the doctor told you to do it to save the regiments lives Turned walking away, "thank you".

I turn up on day five, the injured still coming in, but by about two p.m. it changed to a trickle. By 11 p.m. we were told that only the lucky few shall be coming in now. Then I thought thank goodness what with transport to a hospital and blankets in short supply.

I did feel good, then I told the nurses to go rest and not to rush in tomorrow. The night nurses can help a bit more.

Though the north won the battle; the war was not over. So, the P.X. has got a lot to answer for and where is that new painkiller called morphine I was promised.

Science

In the wonderous out-take of science many wonderous things have been discovered. Examples are the discovery of space travel. First accomplished by U.S.S.R. in 1961. The invention of the artificial heart. Where the first successful operation was in South Africa. Performed by Dr Christiaan Barnard in 1967.

The patient survived for eighteen days.

The invention of artificial limbs has enabled the unfortunate to live a far more enjoyable life. The invention of eye surgery has helped to improve and save a lot of peoples sight.

Different drugs have saved and improved countless lives. Science has enabled surgeons to probe more accurately and perform far better surgeries, thus in many cases giving a longer and more comfortable living standard. Examples are x-ray machines, key hole surgery (where operation is performed by remote control imagery).

Inventions and cures through science have had far reaching effects in our lives, without ! A lot of what we have or know would not exist.

P.S. Note : Many inventions and cures have been created by the perseverance and devotion of the few.

Honestly

In time as humanity thrives on to endorse better than before. Many incriminations and counter claims, a.k.a. accusations are thrown around. All of which prove no fact or have no proven facts.

The only indecision has been made on behalf of insurance companies. Which obscures the reason why person / multi persons died from a pathogen attack.

Hope for those caught up in a disease incantation have never been looked upon as a survival group. They throughout history have always been thought as the ones to perish and suffer, in great numbers. The decision of caring and thoughtfulness has always been given to the next generation.

The downfall of the fallen by protests, bacteria, virus infections has always been recognised as the forgotten past.

Non-contagion

Gather round you little devils, I have another fantastic story to tell you.

Now I want you to know that all your dying and hollering has not been in vain. I hope you live to see the great satisfaction it is to live and die so the next generation of your kind might have the same.

So what we have here in this first part is enough to make the devil twitch.

I am about to think 'thank you' in my mind. When I am thrown (yes) into the dead basket for 2 min 32 sec. Where I am found by a witch who explains to the witch doctor that we have a live one here. So, I look out with death in my eyes and think thanks but no thanks. Then flood the surgery with some leftovers (Ebola).

Then in what felt like years and was. I returned to that hospital and darn it the only one still alive was the good doctor. So, while he sat at his fancy desk. I explained who this eight-year-old kid was. Then I explained to him that he had one of two choices. I have bought with me this gun; you might know it is a favourite of a British officer. I only put six bullets in it. I thought seeing as you humans like sex so much, Ironic huh! So where was I O yes, now I shall return tomorrow, and you can either put a bullet in your head or I shall do it for you. What time do you start work six o, clock in the morning. Nice warm pabbed office you'll be fine. I've checked the bus schedule I should arrive between five past and ten past. Are we clear (yes), louder (yes). Oh and the word thank you for saving my scrawny neck is 'non-acceptable', tomorrow!

P.S. Note: Yap dead, hurrying down the corridor, me coming along the side corridor past the office (screaming nurse, (the Beatles have arrived). I walk up the gravel road to the bus stop and am gone like a ghost I am.

Ah look they have all fallen asleep!

I am trapped in a body. It is a void so in next instance. I was and am on the sea of 'Destiny', on my mission to give hope to the fallen.

Morbidity

- If I am in pain then I shall get through it.
- If I am in agony I shall get over it.
- Customer : Hello, please could I pick-up my prescription. Pharmacist : I'm sorry these items are unavailable.
- I am sorry there is no cure for your ailment.
- Patient : Can you help me I have a life threatening injury. Doctor : Certainly, if you have medical insurance.
- This drug is very addictive an could cause an over dose. So, follow instructions on label.
- Doctor: First the good news, you are going to get well. Now for the bad news the limb shall have to be amputated.
- The longer you live, then the longer you die.
- If I take the drug, will I be alive tomorrow ?
- Patient : As you have told me there is no hope, then what do you suggest next ?
- Doctor : I don't want to but I must let you know that the infection is going to continuously spread across your body until you are dead.
- If I cannot remember anything or how to do anything, what do I do !
- I am dying of living.
- If I keep going to see a doctor for an ailment and asking for different drugs am I creating a split personality.
- What is the harsh reality of more dying from natural causes than usual !
- When will the virus pandemic end

Contagion

Pathogens of the future and the past might be different. But they have one thing in common and that is they are harmful to life.

With the ability to swarm and kill millions.

Though different pandemics have had the ability to de-generise after causing a deadly pandemic. They have not been eradicated completely. They have descended into a semi sleep mode. Then only having an effect when the environment has been programmed for effectual effect.

The pathogens of the future are going to be of a hybrid purity. Meaning the intensity of their contagion is going to be of a highly contagious quality. Being different from what has proceeded them.

It is clear that there has been no divisibility of human knowledge on how to stop the integrity of a disease. Probably as the environment as shown they deserve what they got. Like the past it will be effect before cure. Showing a loss of life before a cure is found.

A important fact shall always be how to contain the spread of the contagion. Then to be able to see how to limit infection. Before worse damage is done. Containment will always be important while a vaccine is developed for distribution to the masses. With the ability of pathogens and diseases to continue to change and infect the environment it does plague upon. The ability to contain and stop a contagious spread of disease infection will always be the important factor before eradication of the germ.

P.S. Note: A very dangerous factor is the thought that a variant of one kind can cause a changing effect. Then becoming a damaging effect of another. But not being of that pathogen cycle.

Defunct

As the horrific super virus continues to plummet planet earth. Killing the humanity and all organic life. As all the horrific things that have happened on the planet come to fruition. As humanity falls to its death a scientist as all things look comes up with a vaccine. Using a radiation mass antidote. From the mass destruction of the earth planet.

Where the neurone anecdotes have evolved to create a beginning DNA.

As I lay dying, I sense what the envision of bird in flight told me. That as the (three gods Sparta, Valhalla, Rome), suns of distance beyond distance align. What is a cure shall be a vision of a new beginning. As I look through the dormatize it after thought explodes and as began.

To ensure the protection of humanity and the future. As the nuclear bombs explode around the planet. They are offset by the planet being of a different view, but still called Earth.

Where off set does not mean extinction but a difference. As the only saviour will be against the weather and what evil do.

Chosen words

I am now prepared and am going in, so remember. Whatever is reported to you your children and the next generation deserve to survive.

If the time-line is what has been calculated. Does that mean the time-line of the future shall remain the same ? When time passes into the future.

I have only half a clear left and someone has to go in and send a report. We need an escape root before time runs out.

It is what you can do for germ warfare, not what can germ warfare do for you.

We need more information because time is running out.
It is just a thought but if we speculate that is a conductor. Then that must be a arial.

Yes I know what you're saying but where is it coming from ?

— which direction
— when will it hit
— what kind of compound quantity
— after initial surge, then how long before we are overwhelmed.
— is there time for evacuation

How did it come to this ?

Do not embrace disease, let it come to you.

Disease is an infection or is it a contagion. Whatever be careful you do not catch it.

Problematic : Always read the label before taking the drug.
Only take required amount of the drug.
What do I do if they runout of drugs ?
What happens if I run up a resistance to the drug ?

P.S. Note : I want to leave you with this ! If what I have said is a lot of fiction. Then what I have discovered for the future is that fiction also ?

Disorientation

With germ warfare and the anilation of multi millions in the past. Examples being the black death that is said to have taken out a third of the human population of planet earth. Then there is the polio virus which is said to have almost destroyed humanity when it was born.

Then came germicide where the fallout of the past deadly diseases. Carried on killing humanity far into the future, far past its initial infestation.

Then there are those that partaked in the creation of diseases. Such as mustard gas where laboratories created an infection that went on to a coveyour belt to create bombs during the great war. Laboratories that create biological infections which they say are for to help in the creation of medicines. Which for all purposes are biological weapons for a quickening death for the human race.

Now, this is a very dangerous aspect of future life. Where you have a virus, germ or bacterial infection. Any which contaminants that think infected have no more to offer. Shall transpire to consider there is further to be had from inter-action with other insecticide.

There humanity creates a dangerous scenario of adding a particle compound to an infection containment that might be on the top of its game. Or a sleeper that has been awoken by particle compound of another to further its expertise.

It is not only deadly and dangerous it is also suicidal to enact upon and think you shall live to see tomorrow. Science is a dangerous fact, that does not care for the future. It just creates and makes claim.

Embattled

War is a nasty situation whichever way you look at it. But I want to explain to you how disease does not stop just because humanity goes to war.

This first fact is harsh but true when in the dark ages and medieval times corpses were left on battle fields for days in fear of reprisals. So the stench of disease infestation was allowed to fester. Where armies would lay siege to castles and be in disgust at what they would find within. A common sign of the plague !

When in the 15th century there were wooden ships. That would travel long sometimes arduous journeys around the planet. A major problem was Typhus. Where the sailors health would deteriorate from the hardship of being on board a wooden sail boat. During the 17th & 18th century when sanitation was not very good in fact very bad in the cities Cholera was free to infest and took many lives. It was a major problem when the infection got on board through infected water. Where it was allowed to spread very quickly. A big problem for naval fleets.

During the first world war a new element was introduced which was mustard gas which killed thousands. With the only protection being a gas mask. When trench warfare was the frontline. Because of the harsh conditions different infections were very common. Such as polio, pneumonia, scurvy. Field hospitals were riff with them, because of the close quarters in the trenches disease spread unchecked. In the orient during the second world war many soldiers caught malaria fighting in the jungles of Indochina. Such as Burma, Philippines, Malay. Where the anti-biotic Quiniean was the saviour.

During the conflict in Vietnam 1962-1970 many returning military personnel were released from duty then came down with what they called a strange disease. Then diagnosed as malaria. Others diagnosed as schizophrenic, suffering from paranoia this was also common in the Persian war after the 9/11 attacks on the twin towers in America. Many combatants lost limbs from enemy fire or booby-traps. Where advancements in cross tactics saw many veterans with prosthetic limbs.

Rechendo

As the earth raves the fire rages, ripping into the hearts of many.

As the thoughts of living are thought the agony of dying take it away.

Where there is a beginning it is proven there is no end.

So much heartache when will I see again. What I can see from my eyes that is not pain. As the dying scream in agony. But the sound I cannot hear, I can but see.

Then I think am I alive or am I dead wondering when will it be me.

How to endure what I cannot see but in every moment is taking a part of me.

With this question I leave thee. How do you endure what is not you. When you cannot see but it takes the most precious from you.

That living so dear to us all.

I live today for what I lived yesterday. But how can I live if it is taken away.

I sleep and awaken and awaken in the shadows of darkness.

I can barely open my eyes.

Then before me I see the grim reaper. Saying come with me to the other side and see in another light.

So I say no but on my own and see through another way. That of death as the light keeps fading on me.

When I leave this place it shall be a wonderous and happy moment.

To leave this a place that as given nothing but 'I never wanted to me'.

Your chains shall not hold me, for I shall melt all before me. Then you shall be none the wiser, as army of death descends and ensures your end.

GERMICIDE

- Accumulation is a aptitude of probabilities, made up of improbabilities.

WARNING this thesis has not been recognized
by any medical body or organization.

Smallpox

Smallpox also known as Black Death was a devastating disease which can be recorded back as far as the 14th century. It is said to have evolved from Europe through decades of neglect and inappropriate sanitation. It spread like wild fire through Africa, Asia and into China. These facts were found to be true from word of mouth to writings of scholars of distinction that claim it got as far as Mongolia in China. It was one of the main stays that started the slave trade of the negro. Where tribes paid for the uninfected to be taken away and the infected killed and their villages destroyed to cleanse the land and stop the spread of the contagion. Homes and villages throughout Europe where burnt to the ground, many times with the infected still inside. The grim reaper stopped at marked doors of homes and shouted for them to bring out there dead. Where they were taken away by horse an cart to be burnt.

The infected were thrown into walled compounds and left to starve and die, but for help from charities. In the end the world just gave up and hoped for the best. Then as if in their final breath a vaccine was discovered by a Doctor Edward Jenner, place of birth England born 1749, died 1823, occupation medical physician. The virus is said to have existed for 3000 years. Evidence found in tombs of Egyptian mummies from as far back as 10,000 B.C.

Typhoid, Cholera

Typhoid is a bacterial infection and the only cure is antibiotics. It is caused by intake of contaminated water or consumption of food washed in infected water. Some symptoms are a high temperature, rash of flat red patches, diarrhoea. It was a big problem in European cities where hygiene was not of a good quality said to be caused by cold and damp environment. In the 15th century it became a concern in many countries, where unknown those that didn't make it were considered weak an unable to survive. As cleanliness in life became a factor it began to disappear. A vaccine was discovered by British pathologist Almroth Wright in 1886. The germ was first detected as a microbe that causes typhus in 1880 by German pathologist Karl Joseph Eberth. The first unconfirmed epidemic of the infection was in 430 B.C., in Athens, Greece.

Cholera infection discovered in 1817, India.

It quickly spread throughout India and South East Asia. It was problematic in the wooden ships of various nations. E.g. Holland, France, Britain. Docksides at the height of the epidemic became no go areas. It was called the invisible killer because no one knew where it came from. It was dubbed the name blue death because of its symptoms. Dehydration, blood thickening, veins starved of oxygen turning skin a sickly shade of blue.

In 1854 Doctor Snow of England discovered the source of infection was bad sanitation.

His tedious efforts ensured new clean pumps where installed and sewers were sanitized.

Particularly in London U.K. a main problem area of disease. A vaccine was created in 1885 by Jamie Ferran, physician (1851-1929) Spain.

Leprosy, Tetanus

Leprosy was discovered by Norwegian Armauer Hansen in 1873. It was the first disease discovered to be a bacteria that causes human infection. With the medicines Dapsone, Rifampicin and Clafazimine a medical cure of multidrug therapy (MDT) was developed in 1960,s. A vaccination as been developed called Bacillus Cadmetti-Guerin ((BCG). First documentation of the disease goes back as far as 600 B.C. There are records of the infection from leopard colonies from the days of the roman empire.

In medieval times 1000 A.D. to 1400 A.D. many leper houses existed across Europe. A stigma against the untreated disease was created because of the disfiguration it can cause.

It is spread from human to human by breathing in droplets from infected through coughs and sneezing. Symptoms are....

Growth (nobles) on skin, Ulcers on feet,

Thick stiff skin, Lumps on face or earlobes,

Discoloured skin (light patches, numb).

Tetanus is a bacterial infection caused by the bacteria clostridium tetani. When bacteria invades the body they produce a poison, toxin that causes muscle contractions. It often causes jaw and neck muscles to lock, lockjaw.

The infection is caused when the bacteria gets in a wound. It is a serious but luckily rare illness. There is no cure for the disease. The infection requires emergency & supportive care. Treatment is clean wound of bacteria, medication to ease symptoms, supportive care. Antibiotics are used to kill the bacteria.

Most cases today (2022) found in central Africa, South Asia. First found in 1500 B.C. in Egyptian documents.

In 1891 Kitsato Shibasaburo a physician (1853-1931) from Japan discovered the toxin that causes tetanus and that it could be treated with antibiotics. Emil von Behring a physiologist (1854-1917) from Poland in 1890 discovered first vaccine against tetanus. In 1924 first tetanus toxoid developed. The tetanus toxoid given to soldiers during world war two has since been recognised as the tetanus vaccine.

Malaria, Leukaemia

- Malaria is an infectious disease caused by the bite of the female mosquito. It creates a very high temperature and creates a problem of sweat & chills, mindlessness, and weakness with other symptoms. Is a very common occurrence in places with a hot climate such as sub-continent, Africa, and Indochina. It was a major cause of illness for the French military of 1878 and during the second world war, got to be known as jungle fever. Returning soldiers were known to have long lasting effects of disease. It is a dangerous disease and can quickly become life threatening. Some people who got the disease were known to have thought to have been cured but again got the infection. Documentation goes back as far as B.C. e.g., Chinese document 2700 B.C. The parasite malaria infection was discovered in 1880 by Alphonse Laveran born 1845, died 1922 in France. First effective cure was the bark of the cinchona tree that contains quinine. Cures are antibiotics such as Quinin sulphate, Atovaquone proguanil and Primaquines phosphate.

- Leukaemia starts in the bone marrow of the skeleton. It moves quickly into the bloodstream, then other parts of the body. It takes just days or weeks to start spreading.
Symptoms are bone / joint pain, weight loss, abdominal pain, low red blood cell count. Cause of disease is inherited with exact cause unknown.
Discovered in 1827 by surgeon and anatomist Alfred Armond Louis Marie Velpeau. Born France 1795, died 1867.
Treatments are Radiology, Chemotherapy, Bone marrow transplant. The infliction can be found in children but mainly found in adults.

Pneumonia, Polio

Pneumonia is basically caused by severe cold such as with thin clothing or bad insulation of homes. It is a big problem for the poor in major cities during winter. Symptoms first discovered by Greek physician Hippocrates in 460 B.C. In 1875 German pathologist Edwin Klebs observed pneumonia bacteria under a microscope for the first time. Which paved the way for many ways to cure the disease. Pneumonia can be either viral or bacterial. The development in 1930 of the antibiotic penicillin went a long way in supressing the infection. Antibiotics are the best way to fight the contagion. There is also a pneumonia vaccine, also known as the Pneumococcal vaccine. The Pneumavac vaccine covers twenty-three different variants of the bacteria. The most vulnerable for catching the infection are the elderly and sick. It is spread by droplets when a infected person coughs or sneezes. It can be caught anywhere at school, work, home...

Polio (poliomyelitis) is a virus contagion which is very contagious. Because of vaccines is now rare. It is caused by dirty hands, contaminated drink and food. The virus is spread through the mouth and through saliva.

A person can spread the disease though they do not feel sick. It usually infects very young children.

Jonas Salk medical researcher born in U.S.A.

(1914-1955) created a vaccine in 1953.

The vaccine was inactivated poliomyelitis vaccine (IPV).

Albert Bruce Sabin medical researcher born in Poland (1906-1993) created a vaccine in 1962. The vaccine was live attenuated oral polio vaccine (OPV).

First epidemic of the virus was in 19th century. Evidence as shown it to be ancient.

Chickenpox

Chickenpox is a virus infection, which mainly infects children, it also can infect adults. Pregnant women are deceptible to the virus.

Symptoms are fever, rash on skin which changes to loose scabs. Takes one or two weeks to be cured. Can help getting better by using creams, antihistamines and paracetamol. It is spread by being in same room as infected or by touching things infected by fluid from blisters of infected.

Earliest known term chickenpox was in 1691.

There is a chickenpox vaccine, which was invented in 1970 by virologist from Japan Michiaki Takahashi born 1928, died 2013.

Diphtheria, Jaundice

Diphtheria is caused by a bacteria. It is also known as the klebs. It was discovered in1884 by German bacteriologist named Edwin Kleb.

It is an infection caused by a strain of bacteria called Corynebacterium diphtheriae toxin. It is the toxin that makes you sick. It is spread by coughs & sneezes of asematic and infected people. It infects nose and throat. Symptoms are throat pain, fever, swollen neck glands, difficulty swallowing.

Nerve, kidney, or heart problems if enters blood stream. The disease can be prevented by a vaccine, antibiotics eythromycin or penicillin.

Jaundice also known as yellow jaundice is when your skin or white of your eyes turns yellow. It can be a sign of something serious such as liver disease in older people. So seek medical help. It is caused by breakdown of Bilirubin the pigment that comes from used red blood cells. A common and harmless condition in babies. Discovered in 1885 to be an adverse effect of a vaccination. The treatment for infection in new born babies discovered by sister Jean Ward from England. Found that sunlight reduced symptoms in new born.

Its scientific name is Hyperbilirubinemia.

Mumps, Measles, Rubella

Mumps ; is a viral contagious disease which causes swelling in the face, salivary glands. Can cause sterility in males, usually gets better on its own. The best cure is rest, fluids, painkillers. It is spread by coughing and sneezes. A person is most contagious a few days before symptoms appear and a few days afterwards. Infection usually lasts less than two weeks. Humans are the only natural host of the virus. Mumps was found in Chinese literature in 640 B.C. Hippocrates documented a outbreak in 410 B.C. Mumps was a major infection during the 1914-1917 great war. In 1945 mumps virus isolated, and in 1948 inactivated vaccine procured. In 1967 Maurice Hillerman a microbiologist born 1919, died 2005 created a mumprvax that is still used today.

Measles ; A viral infection disease which causes fever and red rash with cold like symptoms. Mostly occurring in children. Usually gets better on its own, can make one very ill. Spread by coughs and sneezing. A person is most contagious from the time the symptoms appear until about four days after rash appears. It is considered one of the most contagious diseases ever for humanity to have to face. Described as early as 9th century.

By Persian physician Abu Bakr Muhammad.

It spread like fire through worldwide travel from 16th century. It caused devastation through many civilisations. Until vaccine was procured the virus was endemic. In 1954 John Franklin Enders created first vaccine. Licensed for worldwide use in 1963. In 1968 Doctor Maurice Hillemam improved on vaccine.

Rubella ; A viral disease also called German measles. It is a rare infection. Can be serious for pregnant women. Symptoms are spotty rash which feels rough, swollen glands in neck., aches in hands and knees, high temperature. Last usually about a week. Cure fluid and rest. In 1814 discovered a separate disease from measles by a German named Alfred. F. Hess. Infection caused by a different virus than measles.

P.S. Note : The MMR vaccine is a vaccine against mumps, measles and rubella created in 1967.

It is considered very safe and a life saver against diseases.

Rabies / Scabies / Herpes

- Rabies : There is no effective treatment for rabies. It usually results in death. If infected it is important to have a series of shots.

  Symptoms are itchiness around bite. Might have flu, fever, headache & muscle ache, nausea, tiredness, loss of appetite.

  Death usually occurs two to ten days after infection.

  Three medical phases :
  - Approximately two to four days onset of disease.
  - Excitation, persist to death
  - Paralytic, hydrophobia disappears and swallowing becomes possible.

  Disease known since 2000B.C. First written about in 1930 B.C. Which said measures should be taken against dog bites.

  In 1804 Georg Gottfried Zinke discovered animals transmit rabies., Proven infectious.

  First known human record of infection in 1885.

  A nine year old boy named Meiter. Cared for by Louis Pasteur.

- Scabies : Symptoms of scabies are itchy rash, burrows in skin. pimple like rash. Treatment is creams and lotions. It is easily spread person to person.

  Caused by pestiod Sarcoptes Scabies mites.

  Can occur in two to six weeks.

- Herpes : is a viral disease found in the genitals of man and Virginia of women.

There is no cure for the infection. But antiviral drugs can prevent or shorten outbreak. Those infected have disease forever. It is a danger to pregnant women. To test for disease use a swab sample on sore infected area.

Sign of infection are Itching tingling or burning in vaginal or anal area, swollen glands, flu symptoms, fever, pain in legs, buttocks, or vaginal area, change in vaginal discharge, painful urination, headache, pressure in area below stomach.

The greek Hippocrates first described herpes.

Found to be a viral infection in 1940,s.

Venom

In the world of science there are three levels they are basic, dangerous and hydra.

Basic science = beaker.

Dangerous = fire.

Hydra = transformed.

What is hydra going back as far as ancient time. With the golden fleece a.k.a. the mythical beast watching over.

The hydra with its all-purpose cure dose it exists. Where there are the different many, the potency recedes in a guise of up an up. Where the loss in mental faculties, you must seek medical help is important. It is not that hope as gone away, it is just the usual you cannot see.

As omicron is one I will walk right through you and annihilate your existence.

P.S. Note: You talk the talk but cannot walk the walk.

.

GEMAUGLON

Sexual diseases

There are three major types of sexual diseases, they are hepatitis, gonorrhoea and syphilis.

Hepatitis is the deadliest of the contagion and which in a few months can devastate a community. An example is it is caused by drug infection from dirty needles. There are various infectious kinds of the contagion.

Hepatitis is a virus contagion. It is an infection of the liver caused by sexual contact with infected person or sharing of needles or other implements. There is no known cure, your body cures itself. There are five ratings of hepatitis A,B,C,D,E. It is sometimes called the silent disease.

Aids an off shoot of hepatitis is an infection caused by homosexuality. There is no cure just drugs to hold back the spread and the eventual outcome death. It is highly dangerous because it closes down the immune system. Where when you become highly susceptible to germs and infection.

Gonorrhoea is a bacterial sexual infection which secretes a puss like substance from your sexual organ. It is spread by having unprotected sex. Some symptoms are a sharp pain when passing urine, bright red blood on tissue and itching in sex organ area. There are antibiotic medicines to cure the disease. It is also known as having the clap.

Syphilis is a bacterial sexually transmitted disease. Symptoms are sores on genitals and bottom. The treatment against the infection is an antibiotic injection or antibiotic pills. The spread of the infection is caused by anal, oral and vaginal sex. Also the sharing of sexual toys with the infected. A deterrent being the use of a condom or dental dam during sex.

Ebola virus

Ebola was first discovered in India in eleventh century where snake charmers used herbal sedatives to make the snake lack lustre, but with it being a snake it turned it into a transcending deadly floating virus when released in descending form. It then had the ability to manipulate and destabilise the body form it was setting for, thus creating the chilling epitaph of 'that's all folks'. It spread to Africa because there the people were bad omens and their villages burnt and their lives forfeited. The virus from the toxicity was subdued as a sleeper and the survivor became a carrier. Some escaped on putty boats along the coast of Africa. Now with the onslaught of end game any sleeper cells are mistaking it for a calling. Being able to survive in a foreign shithole because of the essence of whence it came.

With any chance of it just going away being what am I doing in this place? So you can guess the rest, it is a highly agitated virus against foreign bodies so it does squeeze the life out of the host. Which is why froth, sweat and boils from pressure in blood flow occurs. It is wise to burn the bodies before it regurgitates as 'get me more of that fit for it crap'. I have an inclination that it moves on sense of change creating motion drawing it in.

There is no cure for the virus it is having a sense of knowing what to do when it senses you. Mainly don't be around, from here in it is a search for edicacy before it edits you. Highly infectious and any infected person must be quarantined immediately. Area contagion found must be disinfected.

Monkeypox

Monkey pox was first detected in Africa at the end of the ninth century. It was widely thought that because the blacks were cannibals the germ bomb (virus) was created in retaliation against the procreation of the right to life there ends the Negroid.

The virus and its understanding of its mission then slowly spread across all of Africa, the Middle East and into the heart of India. It is said to have reached China along the great silk road. In India it became such a common an uncontrollable fact. It was considered a curse of the Gods. In China along the seafront the virus got out of control like a wildfire. Where 300,000 lives were lost in three years.

Mass genocide and burning of land was enacted to stop the virus. Their thanks went out to Buddha. Many thought they were saved by the Mongolian desert with it burning out the virus with its massive force, and gave it God like stature. To save 11.5 billion people the loss of 300,000 was considered a great victory.

The virus in India and Africa then became a common sight to see on the people.

The virus gives a person the look as if they have spots all over there body. With a symptom being like a cold headache and their whole body covered in a sheet like sensation. In Africa where the virus was rampant many tribes sold out the most infected then eradicated the infected and got rid of the survivors of said tribe. Where we come upon the slave trade between Africa and America.

Where Americans came upon a disease they did not know or understand giving it different names a.k.a. Cholera, Typhoid and wait for it potato disease.

With the invention of the MRA vaccination it was considered a miracle because it miraculously cured Monkeypox. Here the science community was sceptical with half calling it a great saviour and the other half calling it the creation of a sleeper. I was just happy to see a smiling face from the third world where what before looked so scared and rejected. It is now the beginning of 2022 and the virus Monkeypox has returned. With the medical front W.H.O. calling it a state of emergency because of the number of infections and deaths. It is spread by contact with another person. As of 2022 there is no known vaccine for the Monkeypox virus.

It is a disease that takes you to the pinnacle of frustration (itchiness) then decides to either put you down or go away. It has evolved from humanities dis-respect of the environment.

P.S. Note : With the world health organisation (WHO) talking as they are how has this virus transformed on its return !

Covid-19

Covid-19 a very deadly and contagious disease. It affects the breathing system of the body and quickly closes down the nervous system to a point of end of life if said actions are not stopped. It is a very changeable virus which is why, with every new variant, there seems to come more symptoms. Symptoms are fever, continuous cough, loss of mental coordination, difficulty breathing... Doctors have detected over sixty symptoms of the virus. The coronavirus later called covid-19, original strain SARS-CoV-2 was discovered in Wuhan, China. Where in a fish market it was first detected in December 2019. From the first time it was detected it only took four months to spread around the world. Where it has now Infected 100s of millions and killed millions.

Lockdowns, face masks, controlled flow of people all kinds of measures have been used to stem the spread of the virus pathogen.

It has ruined economies and wrecked lives with the loss of so many loved ones.

The vaccine created a year after the infection began has been highly controversial. With the waning of the vaccine months after injection, then booster shots required. Scientists saying a booster program is not sustainable. The vaccine has created some dangerous side effects such as heart aneurism, blood clots, severe aches, pains and migraines. As of 2022 the virus is still highly visible. A system of trying to live with the disease was called for but with each surge it has not stopped the rise in hospital patients.

P.S. Note : Scientists are now at the stage of trying to find a vaccine that will not just stem the flow of the infection but stop it dead.

Health

Ever since ancient times, humanity has been trying to stop the onslaught and ravages of germs, bacteria and viruses.

Such ancient scientists were

Galan 129 A.D. - 216 A.D. discovered link between diet & health.

Hippocrates 370 B.C. - 460 B.C. Systemized

medical treatment. Produced large number of medical books.

Modern organisations that have been created to help stop contagious diseases are;

W.H.O. - World Health Organisation.

C.D.C. - Centre for Disease Control and prevention.

Oxfam, Blue cross, Red cross - wherever disasters or famine have struck they have an obligation to go there and help the survivors with medicines, food and shelter.

Around the world there are various establishments that produce medical equipment and drugs to protect and maintain a healthy environment.

Johnson & Johnson established 1886 produces large variety of drugs and medical equipment.

Medtronic established 1949 makers of a variety of medical equipment.

Angus established 1980 in California, U.S.A.

Provides specialist help for diseases where few drugs are available.

Medical profession employs a variety personnel from Medical administration, Equipment manufacturers, Drug makers, Nursing, Doctors, Drug development, Ambulance service, Pharmacists.

It is a life saver and structure that is a multi-million dollar industry.

Death

Death: when all organs and arteries close down and the substance of life uptake is not possible.

Death comes in many forms as many people suffer and pass and the thought is of another referred to as the mark of death.

Die, an adjective of preference for another's life.

Dies, an explanation of another's passing.

Dying, a thought of victim about its inevitable end or of someone's vision of another's situation.

Dead, when someone is no longer a living viable being.

Died, a graphic description of ones passing.

Death, a glittering description of a moment in time before the end.

Also death is invisible where it is called or comes in another pronouncement, e.g. perished, massacre, slaughtered, annihilation.

It is also a given name in an event when many have died e.g. Black Death

It is even a film star a.k.a. The Rising Dead.

It sorcery is world famous known as the bringer of death. The walk of death. Death walks a crooked pass.

I would die for you, I shall love you till I die.

You might live a long time - pass the bottle -

I died for you. You might say its dead warm, just don't say it's dead hot. It is so mixed up, I am dead mad. You are a dead man, really?

P.S. Note : As striving for life I now understand death incarnate.

Throughout history disease has had a devastating effect on humanity in the 9th A.D. Leprosy was a scourge of the Roman Empire.

Cholera in the 17th century during the age of wooden ships was a major problem on board. Smallpox the Black Death devastated the world in the 15th century. Malaria was a big killer in hot climates. The pressure of such annihilation and society outcry forced the necessity for remedies for prevention to be found.

Clarify

As the Monkeypox disease ravaged Asia and Africa in the 19th - 20th century. Because of its origins China threatened India with annihilation if they did not get control and stop the disease contamination and spread to the Orient. Whereas India in retaliation against Africa for causing the disease spread created Ebola virus to spread into Africa. Then with the discovery of the MMR vaccine the demonic ending of the saga never materialized because it also took out the monkeypox virus, so there was nothing to complain about. Now in 2022 monkeypox has effected over sixteen countries around the world. In the U.K. they claim to have discovered a new strain of the virus. Discovered in 1958 it was quickly to have been found to have infected all of the (third world) southern hemisphere. It is said to have come from central Africa, strongly opinionated by India.

In the 1960,s many diseases entered England through the development of immigration. Negros, people from sub-continent were found to be carrying many dangerous diseases. E.g. Cholera, Smallpox, Typhus. Because people were not used to it. It took on the sense of a bloody Indian uprising. Yes U.K. has had many diseases throughout the ages. But it has strived to eradicate them, and save infected people with medical guidance. It has not dumped their problem on others. India, Africa, Indo-China are major incubators of diseases. Followed by West-Indies and South America. There is only one miracle cure that is get rid of cause of disease.

In hundred years plus the contagion neurone has slept a.k.a. been dormant. Because of pollution caused by industrial revolution and mustard gas during war. Now resources are drying up and contagion that has been lying dormant is waking up and manipulating its ability for aggression. This is causing forgotten diseases to re-ignite with greater ferocity. It has also created a quick sense of kill which is creating a growing mass of death of humanity than before coronavirus 2019 pandemic. Meaning the immune system cannot control or survive natures instinct to survive

P.S. Note : Do these countries that create these shanty towns not want to clear them up because there scared what lies within.

Gemauglons

It is a nice regular sunny day the sky outside is a clear bright blue. With thin shards of cloud spotted about. Then people look up and see what looks like a clear reddish blue bubble floating high in the sky. People ask what is it one voice says 'it is aliens, they have arrived'.

Another says 'it is a mirage created by the environment' and then goes chasing after her runaway dog. Then someone says 'the end of the world has arrived'. Then his wife nudges him with her handbag and says 'don't be silly. I thought we were going to a restaurant I am hungry'.

That evening on the news channel it is reported that a strange amoeba like floatation had been sighted in the sky. The reader also reported various objects of the same description had been spotted over America, India and Africa. The next day they are in the newspaper, with what are the strange phenomena in the sky? News reports were circulating that scientists were racing to discover what they were and most importantly are they dangerous? Satellites were being positioned so a study of the objects just outside the earth's atmosphere could be taken and find out if they were heading towards earth. Three weeks later in an emergency news broadcast the commentator told people not to panic. Saying that the eleven bubbles were heading in earths direction and would crash into the planet in five months' time. Also mentioned that there were strange dot like forms floating within the bubbles. The report signed off with saying that scientists did not know if they were dangerous or not.

In a degree of science I would call them Amibrites with plasmonia within. It is now five months later and the energy pods are smashing into planet earth. People are being told to stay at home and keep their doors closed. Those that have ventured outside there are reports that they are falling like flies, changing into abominations with screams before they died. A worldwide emergency is proclaimed. Millions reported dead daily. From polio, smallpox malaria..... and others. With scientists saying it is all being caused by hybrid germ activity. With the dreaded words a vaccine cannot be expected until at least a year of study and formulation is done.

A year has gone by, the death toll is 900,735,000, sure enough a vaccine to slow the infections is found. Now a search is on for a super vaccine. So people are asking 'will we be around to take it? Will we still have an immune system? Or the energy to take it? A report has been circulating that a scientist has been executed and his family deported for saying we must try to live with it.

P.S.Note : The bubble is a membrionic neurone pulsator. The dots are a mass of plasmonic germaloids. When fusion takes place from the energy impulse touching down on planet earth. The directional finder of the plasmonic will lead forth in what will be as the bulldozer effect.

.

Gemauglonz

I watch as the biological neurone rocket flies high in the sky and instantly pick up my glasses and put them on. Thus doing the same with a gas mask. With a last minute check I ensure all that I can use I have in the sealed place. Then, like less than a minute later, a slow cloud of doom rises in the distance and I think to myself, here comes more trouble.

The body is a bundle of energy with a water source, how to get to you. I am bubbling up as if in a cauldron. I am itching, as like driving me to the unknown of frustration. The connection between the nervous system and the neurone is complete. The dripping like acquisition starts to evolve from instantaneous into my brain, it seeps through the connection eating away at my mind, to what all that is left, is an inclination for food. It has begun the gemauglon syndrome that spreads like a seething search from mind, body to beyond that, which is contagion, to that which what was now is just contagion. There belies the knowledge of knowing of you don't understand. So you must quest beyond to I am fact and that is so, it is not. The birth of the gemauglonz is procured. The infectious must be eradicated because there is no cure. If left to survive they will search to find food. The mind warps, you want it, wants food, end of. With the birth of immunity humanity is still on track for survival.

Gamauglaez

The Gamauglaez is upon us, as we pass over the threshold of one-billion dead. All stability and communications across the world are breaking down. People are being urged to ensure that they report any dead and not to hide the fact. Many areas throughout the world are reporting everything was fine then suddenly within days it looks like a disaster zone. With dead being found everywhere and dying, falling out of their homes.

Masks are being left at all access points and people are being told they are a front line defence until the disease is recognised and serum can be formulated an distributed. All uninfected are being asked to quarantine as quickly as possible. Stores are being riffled for all useful supplies.

The death count is like an out of control train, with no site of when it will stabilize and start to recede. As soon as people are found dead they are being bagged, tagged and burnt. Some countries, where areas are found to be infected, are destroying (burning down) the locality. Lawlessness is rife so protection is imperative.

Science is asking science if they can perfect a razor bomb to cut the neurone connection. Others are looking for a sleeper to protect against mutation, desperate for time to recognise and inoculate with said serum.

Military control is out of control so in some countries civil war is inevitable against the war machine. Retreating to their holdouts thinking people shall die. So gates are being chained to protect against following mutations. Meaning the variant of said disease is at full potency and will unleash finality death throw before humanity mentality kicks in... What mind capability to formulate the pandemic is probably hard to understand in many eyes as one disease would hit then refocus and in time another germ would take its place. As if life is a danger to existence. The most terrifying existence for those caught in the endeavour is probably knowing it was here and is here again. Explaining in its mind and showing how it cannot be stopped.

Gemauglites

In the near future after the gemauglonz attack have devastated planet earth and in the time after they are near on forgotten. Sleepers shall arise known as gemauglites. They are fabricated to look just like the gemauglonz did, but the difference is the kind of germ, virus or bacteria enclosed within the membrane and what are the quantity of the difference. Whatever it is they will be contained in their own embryonic energy cell. What with the energy rising and membrane failing. It will enable the spoors to release and counter attack what is falsifying in its tranquil holdings.

Then it will be a race against time to discover what endangerment has been released. With having to know that they have been gifted with ultimate power of existence. Such as speed, virility and contagious ability. Also a factor is what amount was within the membrane and what are their contagion ability?

You can expect a large number of deaths in the initial out brake. Until it deteriorates in its abilities or is nullified by vaccines or antibiotics. An interesting factor is where is their disembarkation point and where shall they embark to. What is interesting about humanity is it will not be in any condition to interfere.

Fallout

In the aftermath of what has been one of the worst killing fields of all time in death, if not the worst of all time. Countries are waking up as if they have been beaten to an inch of their lives. Food supplies are low but with the worst over shelves in stores are showing signs of recovery. Crime numbers are still high but are beginning to recede as shown in the domestic death count.

Grievances against those that endangered lives through greed and manipulation are high, with people demanding justice. People are demanding prison sentences for people that blackmailed to endanger lives. Natural disasters are a major problem where countries infrastructures are still very weak.

Communities are being encouraged to come together and start to build trust and friendship with each other.

The final death count through official numbers is 1.73 billion lost lives, but adding countries slow on the uptake, third world countries and closed countries, fears are the numbers are far higher. What has been found not possible and untrue has been found to be absolutely opposite. The diseases were more tempered and potent and so riffled the immune system.

Required dose and efficacy was found to have to be changed, which took months. The required amount was then quickly out done with infection rates far out pacing line ups for injections, antibiotics or treatments. Meaning make take because of deterioration effect. In my opinion science knew this but disregarded it because they had no proof.

The truth is people in we must do this and do that is completely shot. All that is clear is when they propagate and hit it, is a fight to the death on the only survival track. How to get over such a terrifying and heart breaking ordeal is going to be a long arduous task.

Coauglaez

In the distant future when people are suffering unto others and the attempts at survival are getting harder to acclimatise because of greed, war, famine and weather anomalies caused by global warming. Contagion will take a new directive but with the same purpose. If humanity persists on creating a habitat for anti-matter to grow, then contagion shall persist on showing the human race where they can get-off. With the formation and materialization of coagulants, which are the perpetual gains of said infection to materialise as variants of said contagion. They are formed in a membrane and effectually grow until they are capable to retreat from the embryonic compound which holds them. Where the compound fluid of the embryo and membrane react to break down the holding. Then the spoors sporadically disperse on their mission of survival, which means death to humanity. They will start with low numbers or big numbers of coagulants depending on the stability of surrounding environment. When they infect if singular it will be like chronological pain of this that and the other. If in groups it will be as if you are being eaten alive.

When it comes to a remedy for survival we are talking about a race against time. Where variants are stealthier and their antigens wiser, then such is what quantity is needed, if more is required later. Then there is what if it adapts to the vaccine and comes back better than before? Let's not fool ourselves, all disasters are fixed as best we can. By working together and not drowning in self-pity.

In their division after the centre fuse of their extrication of fulfilment of exuberance they will confuse into their exponential quest of venture.

Work – out

I am in reality, I have checked the come about and my brain has connected to the surroundings. At the moment I am stigmatized how I entered the faze, I have a very high grade of psylocibin and I somehow am being manipulated to take. The first slipstream I rejected as I don't understand.

It is very apocalyptic, it is dark and I am fazing into the surroundings, wanting only stealth recognition. The gemauglons are in packs and surroundings look like a bombed out fracture, yes that bad ! There is something I cannot see because there is collective signage in each group of gemauglons. I have moved into the shadows of the infected. My move was correct just holding it together the human by the dwindling foot step has been brain stigmatized and is done over until is a wasted particle compound. It is how I suspected heart - mind censorship.

Now my sense is drawing me out which I follow or else I would set-off a signal wave. I am there, I am there at my thought transplant motion. Now I am in stealth and I feel rough. Like the bomb as if I have been ripped apart. I need confirmation, so I set time back motivation. With final word thought you can afford one you can afford another.

P. S. Note : Make no mistake it is horrific and I there has to be a window or it will be a feast you would want to forget without the hangover.

Work – off

I don't know how close you are to a nervous breakdown but if my calculations are correct you should be nowhere there but like a fuzzy kaleidoscope. It is getting close so I am thinking what my strategy shall be. So looking around from within I shall try to sense shadow image, mirror image and an image I shall need for survival outside. I look for a moment then swallow the psylocibin, thinking stealth as I do so. As I step on the reality step forth it comes together. I drop my guard and within I sense, they are too close for comfort. My fears are confirmed mirror image, step, partial shadow.

I want to stay to the end but the weaker it will get. I move forth to searching to find if they have communications. Because they do it is a sense of entrapment. Last sighting motive of wait then so to be the human is no more. I am sure of what I have so I wait it out, seeing catastrophic of what I saw and parallel proof. In stealth motion I am back into feeling very rough to a point things can only get better.

P.S. Note : Science has learnt is again moving on.

Documentation

Without knowing where coagulants are I can only guess they are hidden behind the infected size of the incoming of the gemauglons faction. Whatever the case without physical experience in stopping their enforcement it is difficult in making claim of what shall be their direction of attack. What is needed to counterattack, there DNA manipulation.

It is what has slipped through your fingers and has cost millions of lives!

Time is of the essence.

As you have noticed in a worldwide attack there is nothing to clean up with except body bags. It is people who suffer not the medical profession. What is interesting is that this is the first time humanity has been ahead in the game. They must be well sure of themselves.

Dyphazhia / Ganganite

Dyphazhia : I am screaming with all the nothingness inside of me. Now I am seeking a reaction off tone.

The exponential of my being is forming. Now I am but what am I forming a beginning. I grasp before the senses of what shall be, then they are. I learn nothing but with each timing my sense is not what it was. When all is as is the molten as one procures. I am falling apart and then at the point of dissipation I think divisible of devise and procure of sense of fulfilment. So I go on and the Ganganite is sensed at the final outcome. Then the enormous aroura of what shall be shall be. Call it what you want be the universal sense has fortified for a new beginning and what is you are you.

Ganganite : In the realm of the beginning what other evolvement of the being how procured and how did so in its expertise I cannot decipher.

I can only explain to what one beginning to an end curtail. But the prophecy of time-line make sense.

Explained

Gemauglon

A membrane containing embryonic particles of different clusters of diseases.

Gemauglons

A group of membranes containing different diseases.

Gemauglaez

The formation, action, effect of antigens, attack of the contagion on the human organism.

Gemauglonz

When a membrane is fractured and the formed particles within embryos start surging out spreading the diseases.

Gemauglites

When fractured diseases form together and explode after an incubation period and spread contagion.

Coauglon

Groups of variants of a certain disease encased in a membrane to form from embryos. Which when released are deadly.

Dyphazhia

The inauguration of a beginning of a being.

Ganganite

The beginning to the end of a contagious experience symptoms.

Infecti

The moment a contagion binds with the DNA of an organism.

Bivalent

When a vaccine is created to target a particular variant (omicron) of an infection. Can protect against other variants of disease.

Incident / #1

High there you okay ? you don't look to good !

No to be honest I just tried to do some biz but I got robbed of my money and gear. Now I am stuck in this place. Can you give me a ride up river ? Tell you what help me unload and I'll take you as far as Sasinne. Fair enough if I had known about this place I would never have made the effort. If there not half dead then there like rabid prats. Yae ! you there is the survivors and the mean ugly.

How is your biz, why you like, sure thing ! It's good got one rule know what you doing. Days later, almost there about nine hours. What is it like, what there ? I'm not saying it's a safe place but the death rate looks fantastic compared to the rest of the province. Okay were here, what you going to do ? I don't know look for work. Wow, that's dangerous if you don't get mugged first. I tell you what I'm leaving town here is a $100 bucks. My sail barge is worth $7,500 I give it to you for $750.

But I've got no, don't worry about that. I'll give you the whole works for $750 which I will collect in 3 weeks. If you haven't got the bread I will just toss you off and take it back. I got a ledger with all my contacts follow the rules and you will be fine. But rule number one only take money by wire draft before or just before you deliver. Deal ? yae sure, great it's all yours.

Any hassle don't be proud your,ll find me falling out of the Dead End in centre of town. Good news guys I'm leaving town. If any of you want your welcome to come with me. So you've decided that's great, tell the others meet me here Tuesday in my room. Explain what is going down, okay I get their drift, right if you are having second thoughts now that sounds cool. I've been in touch with the outsiders and they want me to take the country. So I've excepted, you will have to double up your workings or move out.

First we will be travelling through shadow valley, then make a big score in Whimper.

Then blast through to our final destination.

See you soon, word of warning, tough as nails and no talking. For your protection. We made a killing at Whimper $17,000 profit plus the rest. We've been ripping up the country these past nine months. But the gemauglons have reached town. The symptoms are bad like their skin is falling off, eyes as if burning away, pain growing as everlasting if not checked, loss of weight for no reason, temperature over 100°C, chocking and coughing non-stop, I will not lie it's like hell.

Incident / #2

The problem is what with the reports from south of the border and the rest of the world. Communications are starting to collapse, supplies are in short supply. Business is booming, but having to be visible armed to the teeth. People are dying in the street, drugs are going of the shelves like no tomorrow. Hospitals have a reputation of being a death trap. You go in you don't come out is the aroura. I didn't think I would worry about them but I am. Any dead are so contagious as are the living. Their bodies are being incinerated straight away. Medical experts are saying the same thing, we have to wait for it to burn out.

The death count has past one billion, it looks like people are in denial. I walk into town and all I can think of is drugs. Trying any secondary concoction I can. Making notes of any I might need, for front line action if needed. Social standards around the planet are slowly collapsing. With all the drugs and notes I've taken I think I could use the intelligence in my sleep.

P.S. Note : This note is far into the future, over the minds of the before which have been confined as to mythical truth. Where the aroura of your breath in out or you do not breath. You are beginning not to think of the terrifying numbers of dead and dying. You are sensing it is normal. You are thinking what of the future, can I get there, that is something new.

Observations

What you are about to see are observations to ask yourself when looking at the frontline of anti - matter.

- How many gemauglons shall there be.
- What speed shall gemauglons or coauglons be moving at.
- Where will there first point of impact be on the planet.
- What shall come first coauglons or gemauglons.
- When will the double strike happen.
- Which type is more lethal.
- When identified which is more important to stop first.
- Will they all come together.
- Where will a safe place on the planet be.
- What kind of mortality numbers are you looking at.
- How long to bring serums up to speed.
- Will there be surges.
- What is human life span expectancy if infected.
- Will it affect the quality of the food chain.
- Will the effect on people be different from one continent to another.
- What caused the abomination to appear.
- Is it human developed.
- Should I be worried about advice given by government and scientists.
- Should I have a cocktail of pills to protect or stem the disease spread ability.
- How do you recognise one gemauglon from another.
- How do you recognise coauglon from gemauglon.
- Will it affect animals.

Rip-off

I will not suffer to enter the world of the gemauglons. So I sit cross legged on the ground and throwing my spirit world forth, as I descend I think hope, peace, love.

It is bleak, then suddenly I am in a sense of turmoil. I am ripped apart into bits, I am in uncontrollable agony. I then come into thought right and recognise the dividing line between life and death. I have now a sense of being here but I am there all with a sense of anguish. With the tensity rising and falling in its wake as if searching for a height. Then when it finds it is like a repeat sequence. With the tensity of each on a highest. With a reckoning ' it is as it is '. Then a moment, then a terrible ripping apart sense of loss. Then as the agony slows down like in slow motion watching myself come together. Then like a rising it looks an says ' you are not one get stuffed '. The dwindling away I did not understand. Now with the agony of thought an trying for one to retrieve myself. I understand exactly the agony & ecstasy I seek.

P.S. Note : As if indicated to say, 'You must ascend to the top of said hill before you can descend. So I descend to the top of said hill, before I ascend off said hill. An underground protocol of the Orient of will anybody survive.

Demonic

It as happened the stuff of nightmares has evolved. The super disease has evolved on planet earth. The strange contact has been made with a digitule contact. With Gemauglons sweeping from the North and Coauglons sweeping from the South. With just a miniscule slowing of motion as they infect and some more when they cross. The deadly entrenchment of the attack to infect is of the same. Because the spread is of float not antigen evolvement.

The rush to get serum up to speed is on. Nothing but complaints about how quickly will it be available. Now comes the major logistics problem which has infected who and to what effect. Slowing the help time-line to a snail's pace. Which some would say is like looking at a death sentence. The quality of the main stay of self-diagnoses is becoming the most important must have, along with remedies an protection. Then naturally the word starts coming in that they are sold out. Hospital numbers are drastic, so people are being asked to self-medicate. So infection is getting worse, for many very bad an death is there only friend. A terrifying aspect is that the contagion is at its ultimate. So is infection by contact, by air and after death. It still spreads as incubation, accumulation and infection is still possible. Scientists are working hard but nothing they have is stopping the effect of viable infector.

The only fact is the east west effect has had a perfect effect or bombastic effect. Things are desperate people are screaming for help out of windows, people dying in the streets. With authorities insisting bodies be burnt quickly as possible. The only hope is to slow down the infection spread with secondary cure (over the counter remedies). Until you can get help from doctors and front line serum.

There are so many people getting infected the help ratio to save ratio is getting farther apart. Hold out until contaminants burn themself out is all important.

P.S. Note : With the North South, East West effect . We are seeing a clear sign that what is needed is a super cure to irradicate said not bacteria, germ, virus.

Anti-matter

Hello, High, G,day are all a form of greetings.

So what does that make anti-matter. Nothing but a non-way of bringing up conversation.

What is the definition of anti-matter ? It is a form of compound but is not. Example if you have one, then you have parts of one, but you have parts of many.

You may not understand calling it a load of gibberish. Then it will just go right over your head. Now we have established that a gemauglon is a form of anti-matter. I want to take you into their world and show you what they think of seeing you space. They see your world for some unfortunate reason. In your case sometimes tragic reasons. It is a boring non-conforming attire, that denies the right to existence by solidification. Which leads to the destruction of reality by greed and want. Somehow in this world a reaction takes place which creates a solid thought of process, that does not conform to the reality of existence.

This is where the solid form to solid existence takes place. Causing a destruction of without from within. This form of solid which I see as a sleep mode is a strange new world so it will makes of it as will.

The dividing consequence of the escaping anti-matter is what creates the want and destruction of organisms. Because they are in the way of improvement to seeing change of the antigen.

Now we have established a protocol of why you existence as a bit of a problem with existence. This is where science can play an important part in trying to save the time-line from torture, horror and terror petrification.

Through these resources without, within, without / within, within / without a form of coequal existence must be created.

There belies the problem ! How to when one does not recognise the other. It is a world of problems, where to find the answer is the question. Especially when time is of the essence.

Nu + 0 + A

So, I have just figured out that the best way to stop an onslaught is to find a remedy. Ah here comes the mad scientist. Now be quiet because that is all you can do and observe. Dressed in his attire it puts on its dazzling long white overcoat. Commencing the ritual (to self). Looking down the microscope I can't believe how it is taking so long, here let me take a look, ah yes, I forgot the specimen. So, after two cups of coffee and grooming its hair (non cholantly). He picks up the beaker with the pirate on (meaning danger) and picks up the vile (upside down) and pours liquid over floor. Then speaking in honour (himself) the flag rendition of the flag puts gently it thinks (not) beaker and vile, spilling more specimen on its bench. Then goes to cupboard marked cleaners and takes everything (throws in motion) out. Then spends ten minutes trying to configure what it needs and ten minutes how to use it.

Then pouring everything out of containers in cupboard into bucket adds one-eighth water. Then proceeds to use it over the contaminated floor. Then going to cupboard puts on plastic gloves and picks up the polish cloth and dips it in the bucket to clean lab top. Forty-five minutes after cleaning lab bench and looking not sure if bugs could be kept out. Spends five minutes looking at himself in the tap in case there are contaminations. Then carries on using pinchers from vile puts speck on glass plate and slaps other on top. There seeing nothing tosses used plates to one side. After the lab top looks like a brawl in the new world, I try and adjust scope as the professor looks down the microscope and declares result and mutters that is what persistence, hard work can get you. As days turn to months, he puts a specimen on slide (I decide to help giving it this and that we I mean that it parts like rage incarnate). And the good professor looks at it and thinks this is bad, it is devisable by one.

Then the director (with his beautiful red face walks in). So, professor I see you have been working (hard) up a grant as usual. Yes, and I am desperate to get a report on your desk. Then I am sure you will grant my funding for a magic wheel.

P.S. Note: It is a honour to know how tireless scientists have strived for nothing but a handout to help others.

.

Aftertour / #1

What a sight baron sight ahead of me. Baron sight behind baron all around. Enter a town it is like a dust bowl. I am looking south coming to a town. Where it looks like creeper virus has not took to yet.

We have a set pattern if we see a town. What we have to trade we hold back on the outskirt of town. Then with three of us go to town, the others hold back watching our backs in the shadows. Our unwritten rule is ' if it is not infected then it is occupied. We are lucky we have a good group of wheels hummies, modified four by fours and motorbikes.

Yae ! an most important armed to the teeth. Oozies, napalm grenades, high velocity rifles. The three go in and they will trade for food today. For a quarter filled case of diamonds and jewels. So deal done they get the quarter filled treasure chest. We get seventy-five cans of long lasting nutrition.

The scouts did return with disturbing news that a war was coming. Outlanders were sweeping down from the north killing and pillaging for supplies. They were not taking prisoners. So that night we decided the buck stops here and we fight. So heading to the coordinates. Hundred miles to the east we meet up with the leader Peter and his woman Martha. So returning to camp I explained the situation. He mentioned a vast army of 100,000 was coming. That 25,000 us where here and when the enemy arrive we are hoping for 40-45,000. We if it is a war then they shall come. Or they die and what little they have would be gone.

Sure enough two months later when they came there were 39-43,000 of us and still coming. There was hope that when the fight began the noise would bring more. Our front line was mortar fire and long range assault rifles. Our main force in the brush about hundred yards back.

So that evening the sway of a vast army 100,000 plus rested and slept. The following morning when they started to rise. We opened fire with mortar and long range rifles.

Aftertour / #2

The battle went on for two days but we won.

Getting into finally man to man combat, pushing them back. We chased the remnants over the river. We had won at a cost out of our twenty-seven thirteen were dead.

On the third day we cleaned up burning the bodies in a lime pit. We were taking no chances ravaging what was of use. We had to move quickly for body smell draws in the virus creepers... On the fourth day I went and said good bye to a great leader. He assured me he knew the situation and would be doing the same.

The virus war is a different story.

You do not know they are upon you until you are dropping dead from its savagery. So as I returned to the gang where we are a strong a unit as ever. As we moved out the virus was I thought in a different ending. The best weapon against it was a spot gun. Then locate and use fire on them. Using disinfectant lookout for fusion bomb reaction. If they are on the hunt they explode the frontline. One spot on a spot gun was say a billion antigens, five spots five billion. You fight you live at speed or die trying. Where remember the few is the sign. Spot guns are the prize, make a lot selling and the more you have the safer you can get. Stop them before they can attack an multiply into greater numbers is the game.

When the coauglon hoard and the gemauglon swarm meet it was a fusion bomb of mass capabilities (they would not have stood a chance). That just sort out survival, and end what was human extremities. A great hope was the VR-3 vaccine that when activated in the human system around the creeper virus.

Creates a stinging sensation that decapitates particle evolvement. But the problem was the same mass creating, but you were alive. Only vaccine deficiency was the problem.

That is worth a ransom where kept in a secret science location which had strength in protection.

Now we were loaded and had trade for a living to contemplate. We also had our lives to be thankful for.

P.S. Note : O yae ! an a prize gift from the cap, n A weapon of mass destruction a spot gun.

Aftertour / #3

Driving sitting contemplating how did we survive. The strategic onslaught of the outlanders, clearly an attack in numbers to create a nothing number.

We clearly from intelligence knowing a superior number coming at us took on a plan of tactics.

As the frontline fired mortar and long range guns. Timing was important as the frontline fired, with enemy getting closer the second wave moved up to greatly intensify accuracy of firing. Then there holding the third wave went in.

Now a major force of tactics took place with moving forward to again increase fire power and accuracy. The two groups of the third wave split and started to create a wave of fire on the unsuspecting outlanders. Using a crushing effect down the side lines. The tactic working surprisingly worked a treat. So shot to bits then the two forces meet surprise and frontal attack completed the victory from the jaws of defeat.

As we moved along the dust bowl of west to east we came upon encampments. Which was good to see holding their own. The towns were considered as scorched earth with virus creepers lunging and searching for pray. Only the hardy survived if they were lucky. So go figure what was within was there quality to have. With survival, shadow movement, avoidance all-important the prize was worth the effect. Supply and demand was survival.

Within the boarder of Texas and Mexico an ignition point of a virus meeting. The only thing left is now virus creepers and a deadly fight for survival.

So we swept on west to east where at Apache pass was noticed upon an ingenious way of protection from the virus creepers. Dug into the red mountain side sealed buildings. Where holdings of disinfectant and medical surplus could be stored. Where we traded guns, disinfectant, knives and implements for cans of food. Where we had done good as we prepared to move on I suggested we start dropping hints of what the ladies would like for themselves. So heading on beginning to sweep north past D.C. We knew we were moving from danger to killing fields. But we prevailed trading with the wise and shadow walking in the in the virus vines. By the time we reached west of Michigan we had disinfectant and food so decided to head into the heartland a.k.a. Badlands.

So after a wild party of what little could be remembered. What lies ahead ? Answer nothing but the same unless one of us cracks.

If the planet stagnates like it as, hen what will change it ? What a mind boggling thought. Another thing the booze it's got to get better this Yazz is old school.

Aftertour / #4

There is something strange about being out in the Badlands. The virus creeper is prying the heart out of all the compounds. With the effect of a deadly contagion somewhere in time - lock in many of what the virus vines took out. When we finished circulating it was a confusion bomb. With a read out give it your best shot, I would not miss if I was you. About the infectize I have read it thoroughly and each has a different annihilation code. Its centralized code is if you do not take yourself out. The common compound of infestize will sort it out for you. We entered to fortify our true existence and what is left of us will get this through drop by drop, there is no other way. With the wave of time preparation of two to four minutes. It is important that the aroura of divide and hold is maintained. To give solidified a chance to signal it is burning. Then rage in and burn it out. a.k.a. it does work.

It is very unfortunate with full blown infection the asymatic kicks in and mass murders take place. So it is important that they die with what they have done for its creation. Or they will murder to make confused connection.

Beware then the richest on the planet shall be cleaners. Those monsters that you see in your mind and think you don't want to see are them. Really they are real, they shall arrive so going to sleep or want another ! It was fantastic in those last four minutes before the world died. Knowing that they were washed up and it was mine, now I am so. 'How to get ya, whatever that is.'

Biontic experimental #1

BIONTIC EXPERIMENT

The experimental biontic configuration is about to be conflagrated into defermental dyphalizisation of demenial contentuose dissolve. Passing devolvement is now experdentially damaged to conforge that systemial depridation of the formationist homoniest is consized convolved. Now distorted vision of dissolve is climatized by disinvolved can be comatozed commencement into the next phazical of before completion.

It is recommended reconciled that all dissolved humanittized be confirmed confine containized as humerical alive confirmed as alive was unbiastansiated as nessacary.

The phractastencial of dissustant is defuse as tracterialize ievozige to exstentize cagioulist cagulize effectizedic as best utilized defurnatinize to solidizique confisticized cofirmalatez. Then preaduledue evolvent to aevolvexedist to confine holaizeded vastinze, gemakrical, Bioacricationz. Upon instelasided draphilationed to contuosize venimouses constrictoned.

Those the nyalistihyz ashas defunctulize validaization of said valulizations. Dispersserized as invalidist depravation.Could be dangerous so should be ostrisized to provicate compondable professionalizi of others is compels. Drugizisz influmations for nyalistias detemental to survivistic time-loop destabled loss. Destablize inedentize wrong forstaling the massignites. So nothing best stigmatizic until thurulized gone dwelled safe as. Bevevalize steristicized strictnize disposition for innocenses.

P.S. Note : Through this most impossible terrifying experience to complete sanction of the human race to keep them well for the rest of their lives. An to conform to responsibility for the best possible hope for the next generation.

Horrificest

With the collapse of the right to life divide of the north and south hemisphere there has been an unprecedented amount of contagion created in the clean north by the third world south. The respectability of life has gone from high octane to disease incarnate. The filth and squaller creation instead of normal development has spread to the north hidden under the guise of immigration and refugee status. Which I consider having a hidden agenda of 'destroyed their homeland now it is worthless. Have created a terrorist chain track. Fronted by paralytic terrorists. As the standard of living deteriorated in the southern hemisphere since 1932. It has now reached the northern hemisphere. Where rapid deterioration of a decent lifestyle is disappearing rapidly. Only Russia and China are holding down some kind of decorum of survival.

Once England fell the third world has been entering Europe in numbers of tens of thousands. Where England is containing as a terrorist state Europe is heading for mass genocide. In the western hemisphere too late for them they have found without natural growth their lifestyle to is on a Armageddon course. The price of pittance that grows in its backyard now costs millions. Just to insure a roof over their head. While squaller around them forms like an avalanche. With south America heading towards a dust bowl by following in the footsteps of their ancestors.

They are pulling the U.S. with them.

While the quick destruction of the planet keeps on picking up pace survivalists are frantically searching for agents in space with news of a survival track. With a nuclear strike only being held back by the ferociousness of the south and north poles.

If they fall only a nuclear strike will be able to stop a havoc of contagion. That will lead to an implosion of the planet and extinction.

P.S. Note: Just because of greed, those that beg for mercy shall be the first to die. In the eventual fifty years after the peak of surviving gives up on what was once a nice place to visit. The planet earth shall be no more.

Sign off

What is going on here it is so hot. This is the sea where is the breeze. It's been almost a month, put the flag at half-mast before I forget, water supply is running low.

We have lost five mates so far and everyone is feeling half their normal speed. Still no breeze or cloud in the sky.

I have decided to do it their way and so we are cleaning the boat as best we can from aft to past. That was like climbing one of them google eyed mountains. No problem I was so sure we got out of there in time. But I guess it had breached the wall.

This is bad another three have fallen. So, I have made a decision that we shall bury the three at sea and in the morning try floating our way out.

It has taken almost all morning to get the tugboat and supplies onboard. Lost another mate also, but my mind is made up we go.

So feeling so weak we could hardly eat anything at breakfast. We lowered the tugboat and with what was left of our strength we looked and said goodbye. Then raising the sail, then drifted off.

I thought on board was bad, fever felt like the sun was stealing our treasure. We didn't do so sod good very good. As like a ritual one by one we fell overboard to protect the others.

When I left I said and put the axe by his side.

"You know what to do think contaminated".

Then climbed away.

.

Biontic Experimental #2

Botanical Experiment: The experiment of diagnosing the diagnosed into a siterial dehydrate to be discarded as waste.

Passing attack of the convergence of damage is now at human endurance. Now human must be flatlined to be revised as to cured.

It is advised that all humans that are revived be confined, observed, and restrained if necessary.

The use of pharmaceutical compounds is ill advised. In the procurement of survival once revived. The cabalistic compound could be harmful to the effect of full stabilization from effects. Drugs might induce physical inequality. Then the breakdown of motivation abilities.

Causing adverse effect would or could make individual dangerous so must be confined.

To protect others in survival mode.

Drugs would cause mass distortion in the anatomy, as patient is being nursed to health.

Drugs must only be used in emergency while the reviving process is in motion until free from effect. Givers of formula must be patient to protect the innocence.

.

Obituary

As a child at my mother and father marriage ceremony. About to have my photograph taken, with them sitting in the background. I remember I kept on thinking to myself. I do not want to do this. Then as the photo was taken, I felt like I wanted to die. I want to kill myself. Then I started looking and walking around as if in an empty space. When I came round, I felt as cold as death. Thinking this is where I want to be and if I cannot, then I flatlined myself.

Awakening in the throes of death.

(Mutilated into pieces of nothing over and over). But I didn't care it was where I wanted to be. I was beginning to understand it.

Then I awoke in another place and started blasting forth like a Gemauglon. Setting to their standard one particle after the other. Then finishing it with a biological blast. Which took me to my existence.

Then I awoke in the frailty of human sadness and got blasted to another place.

Where I buried myself as a nutzoid in alcohol & drugs.

Then burning out on that I wiped out on education and preparation to perish.

P.S. Note: I cannot say if I am happy or sad. But I can say living came in different ways.

.

Conspiracy

Hello, high my name is me and now would like to introduce myself as I.

You can take the following words of a mad scientist (creates nuclear bombs). A crazy man (found something it has no control over).

A nutter (obsessed with something but just can't put its finger on it). Whatever, it's a thriller that took all time and space to create. This is a true and precise account to the best of my knowledge of anti-matter. When the great deluge of infection crashed into the rift of space it created life on earth. There was mumps, rubella, measles giving the nervous system. There was cholera and typhus giving the skin cantation. There was leukaemia giving the senses. There was leprosy, tetanus giving you a heart. There was smallpox which gave you your mind. There was pneumonia, polio which gave you blood. There was malaria what gave you rest and sleep. There was chickenpox which gave you thought for feverment. These are all facids that created the beginning of time before life was created. We also have Ebola within it. There is monkeypox a menial moment. There is covitesz a reason to survive.

All are just a speeded-up process of your human life existence.

Now I have your attention let us get into a wonderous science phenomena (before it gets hungry). So, taking all the above we have an accumulation of creating something. Then we have the Mary Celeste where the horror of being was so intense (growing so intense) they gave their lives for the flag. Then we have the tireless doctor sawing, ripping, giving all, it can. To understand an explanation why a soldier would want to live or die in a civil war. Then we have redskins that insist the medicine man give them a base-line existence. Then we have the incantations which all mean the same thing (infectious). Now as a matter of fact we have how we can get wrong and right to be a whole as to say. There we have a wonderous creation, (because it says so). Through development with particle compound (0 + A =) or with the mind (theory test).

When the good doctor was not one of those that would walk away and found the cure for smallpox with the magic wheel.

.

Glycerine

The thunder rages and the lightning strikes.

Then the centre of disease control,(CDC).

The federal drug agency,(FDA). The world health organisation,(WHO). Announce the gemauglon disease outbreak has reached pandemic proportions.

Doctors, Nurses, Paramedics are being overwhelmed. With the sick and dying patients far out numbering the beds availability and adequate medical care. A added factor being announced that medical staff are quickly getting sick and unable to perform medical duties. Then becoming patients themselves.

Scientific mandate have just made a report on what shall be happening over the next five to ten years. The report states that there shall be five or six massive waves. Of the gemauglon contagion with intermittent waves of the gemauglon bubble in between.

Medical facilities will be over run and large buildings shall need to be commandeered to accommodate the infected. Vaccines for the infections shall quickly become in short supply or non-available. If not ineffective in retracting the combined effect of the gemauglon infestation.

Security will be paramount and the infected must be inoculated first. To stem the spread of diseases. Cross infection between person to person will be very easily sequenced. The contagion of the disease will get more infectious as the years pass by.

Normality must be sustained as much as possible. Even though its existence shall be near non-existent. Reports on the infection should be kept to a calm responsible voice.

Meaning not to be out shone by the horrific truth of the matter.

The worst is expected to last worldwide for a decade and start to retract in year eleven.

The number of dead will be in the billions and the number infected will be greater. The sheer scale of the catastrophe even though it is coming clear people will not want to know.

They shall just want it cleaned up and forgotten.

The source of the virus will be the mystery topic. With many saying it was a myxomatosis of contagion. Picking up toxicity as it moved north. Then spread on planes and ships throughout southern and northern hemisphere.

Whatever, the possibility of survival is now on a downward spiral. To a non-possibility of living on the planet. With the possibility of survival for humankind then passing to other life forms & plant life. Causing the failure of crops and the diminishing of food stocks.

Anarchy will become the fear factor for living. But also a quickening toward extinction.

Gemauglon War #1

The satellites of observation & communication slowly circumnavigate planet earth. The dreaded inevitable has been observed slowly getting closer to the planet. The gemauglons approach in their multi-billions. With their flagship of truth waving forth with an omen.

'You have and were given the chance; you now face the consequences of your actions'.

The deadly rays of the ionosphere have taken out millions. But with recuperation and catch-up the view looks like none. Within fact non-quintessential.

Now having entered the atmosphere. They are just hovering in inner space. Whereas earth command has been wondering what next. Knowing that toxic intrigue would just cause a negative effect. That would grow in expediential velocity causing turn out of human waste. I suspect they are thinking gemauglaez divide and then exterminate.

If the gemauglon knew what they were thinking. The attack on planet earth commences, picking up speed. Hitting planet earth at 700,500 m.p.h. They then divide into explanation coauglons. Collecting on numbers from multi-billions to trice magnitude in hours. With the area of topography mapped out from their mind to the inevitable. The battle to the end of planet earth had begun.

.

Gemauglon War #2

Within hours across the world hospitals are reporting expediential numbers in disease infection. To the best of their knowledge humanity has been preparing by making all toxic medication facilities vacuum tight.

So with the hope that supplies of anti-toxins and vaccines have been procured a chance to survive. Within weeks the planet is looking like a virus / bacterial disaster area. Many nations are keeping in the back of their mind the required necessity of liquidation of over run.

Infected areas before they turn into an incubation area or transactor area.

Underground areas of high technological are like gold dust and highly sort after.

Radar teticon guns are being used to try and stop the spread. But persistence is ravaging their technology knows how. With each take out their knowledge of know how is getting more easier to be sussed.

The devastation is being found to be thorough and common. Very quickly it is becoming obvious of very quick liquidation of all that is in the attack area. Because of the capability of the pathogen to regenerate in infected areas. It is getting in comparison for areas collapsing like the domino effect.

Humanities infrastructure is failing. The thought of liquidation and genocide is quickly being put to the sword. Biological warheads are being exploded around the world. It is getting harder and less possible for the dead to be collected and disposed of. There is also a massive problem in getting proper care for the infected. Danger is inevitable with so many asymptomatic and systematic people. Whichever they are possible for finisher climatises to them.

The bond of suspicion is being spread by numbers. So, it is not long before genocide raises its ugly head. In the guise of protection of boarders. With the demise of liquidation and annihilation. The race is on to get a super bomb together for release. To disintegrate as the saviour of planet earth.

Another strong antidote has been the makers of protective clothing and oxygen contained containers. Said facilities are being added to the other vacuum protected areas. As the world screams mercy, which is a word of no understanding. Pestilence and suffering are becoming a long normal torturous consequence of asking for the inevitable.

Gemauglon War #3

The demise of humanity is slowly getting worse. Passing the deadly mark of over one billion dead in just over a year. Now three years later the number of dead is closing in on two billion. There seems no way to stop the gemauglon attack. Vizon weapons and trecton guns are becoming the new race for super weapons. As the world falls the design, making and use is a don't think twice. Simply because there is no time. It is getting impossible for humanity to connect with each other. Because normalized and caring is getting hard to believe or understand. The word trust is just a minimal compound.

The problem with all these terrifying new weaponries is that it does not kill the pathogen.

It just sends it on its way to a new area. Where it joins in the chaos and destruction in that area. Creating a quickening of destruction and growth. With search and destroy becoming more genocide and lethal. The urgence of finding a vaccine bomb is getting more desperate. With an annihilation bomb just destroying humanity. With the pathogen just moving on. Because of humanities uncaring ways.

Gemauglon War #4

The planet earth has been totally destroyed.

Life expectancy without proper protection or medication has been put at one week to one month. As planet earth reaches the atmospheric intensity of 'The Killing Field'. The science and scientists of survival have finally obtained the knowledge to create a vaccine bomb. So somewhere in a secret location where the earth is about to be changed forever. The application for humanities survival is put together. An almost like conveyor belt of vaccine bombs are created.

As drip by drip timing, droplets transition and component visibility is connected. The firing pin will be a timing mechanism of liquidation.

With the divisibility of division and necessity. Then without the only chance would be sleep and existence from once where.Then if I am right, it will be back to normal (work, party, want) for humanity.

P.S. Note: As the gemauglites succeed into outer space and the aroura turn to sleep mode for this is. What human see is it as is not of their knowledge. But they are so a flag shall be raised drawing in those that helped shall be drawn in.

.

Plan of Decimation

What does the unacceptable truth of the future hold for humanity. Where every which way and that they turn means more problems.

The problem is if they are not a small problem, they cannot handle it.

The covid-19 virus pandemic has only slowed up so as to recuperate. To improve its chances of annihilation of humanity in the next surge.

Food prices have been hijacked to the extent of unaffordability. Affordability is vastly being out paced by cost-of-living prices. Meaning that famine is vastly approaching.

The cost of amenities with oil, gas, electric, is being made near impossible to pay price for. That mean quantity for use is being drastically depleted.

All in all this mean general living standards are on a downturn. Which mean those in the right place are not going to change. Those that can pay survive happily to die. Because the masses cannot pay to survive. Meaning the quality of living will quickly diminish. Because of unaffordability and unavailability.

Which means riches for the few until the masses are needed for progress or not.

The only winner in this sorrowful I'm its saga will be petulance, disease, famine.

Which will thrive on capability and vengeance. Whatever millions of dead will look like pittance. Because of weakness and frailty caused by the diminishing of the immune system.

P.S. Note: The sign that action counts more than word. Shall be when payment of cost at general standard is not adequate for what was paid. That mean in just over a year affordability of living is not possible for you and your family. Taking from other relations will gain you months. But your dept will be up there.

Parathegon

Skylab was created and sent into space in the 1970, s. It was a very controversial mission. Where the U.S. was accused of carrying out dangerous biological experiments.

Here are the findings of said report from Skylab satellite, as you can see it is quite thick. Which for the good of planet earth place where experiments took place is now non-operative.

Skylab was first visited by Skylab 2. Which was carrying the deadliest pathogens known.

Both bacterial and viral sealed in lead containers. The pathogens were Malaria, Polio, Typhoid, Cholera, Smallpox, Leprosy, Leukaemia, Pneumonia.

On Skylab they were placed in separate vacuums, then the lead sealant was parted.

There was an outer seal of lead for each compartment a security precaution. What they recorded was astounding. It not only proved the ability to live in but also to revive in space. At first it looked like they had died. But when brought back into an oxygen environment they suddenly showed motion and activity.

The instrument panels reading of weight, size, power, growth was fluctuating from .01 to .08 / .09 This revival was clearly an entity of amazing if not possibly terrifying ability. Considering just rest and sleep required for growth. They were then mixed with sugar, milk, and treacle. With each time devouring their host.

The second part of the experiment was carried out by Skylab 3. This time sealed all together in two lead containers. They were again released in a space vacuum. With mesmerizing results. So horrific the readings showed again sleep time revival with readings .8 / .9

With energy capability doubling. With again devouring mater of jam, peanut butter. and bread.

The other container contained same amount of pathogens with same experiment process. But was mixed with same matter substances as Skylab 2 experiment Sugar, Milk, Treacle.

The purpose of Skylab 4 was to dock at Skylab 1 station and collect all monitoring data then return to earth. Then to compare data with Skylab 2 & Skylab 3.

Then the most dangerous part of the mission was enacted. The burning up of Skylab in re-entry to earth atmosphere. Which unfortunately was not complete, where unsubstantiated parts did not burn up. Which allowed through sleepers, which are now awakening. Where you are getting these unsubstantiated outbreaks of germs.

Nuronotics

To understand anti-matter, you must first understand why upon this planet earth. You must understand where and when they did first strike. To further their existence on the planet. When you consider each mass evolvement. You then realise how they arrived on the planet in one cycle.

Then fading with each strike leaving one pathogen dominant. While all others phased out to neutralization. Then from beginning of the planet until present day they evolved dominance to obscurity. With a forgotten after effect.

As they formed factual content on the earth they did divide past present through phasing in outtakes. In various frequencies Polio outbreak, Pneumonia outbreak, Smallpox outbreak, etc.

Now the times are changing from belief in division to time of awareness. Where tactical understanding and safety will become a priority for survival. If you can understand the ferocity of a newfound pathogen. You can understand how deadly and uncaring they can be to anything that does not understand them.

You now realise how important that safety and proper actions are a necessity for survival. Where incompetence just enacts a greater loss on humanity. How effective or ineffective would the knowledge of the past be in the future. What would be the damage to humanity on its arrival then fades. As their abilities far outweigh any human effect. What would be the consequences of any human interference in a pathogen attack. What will be the prospect percentage for survival. Would the planet be able to survive through further time lapses.

Will the division between humans and survivors still remain a neutral factor through time. Will the more learnt keep a divide between present and future. Or will genocide ambiguity be able to grow. Or the strength of divide stays intact to protect the next generation. Would an obliteration bomb become powerful enough to outsmart the planet intelligence. Will it be possible to stop the effect of global warming. Causing the effect of evolvement giving pathogens sanctuary. Because they are a single entity, which is something else in focus.

The truth of nepotisms is in many words as is amplitude. They are both I'm it factors that can sustain a fixation of an urge. How you die or live through it is just you.

There is no doubt that vaccines and antibiotics (MMR, Penicillin, Quinine) etc are a competent effect. But waning treatments just give a weaker anatomy to infect. Eradication is the best possible survival protection. Then there is no variant change of effect.

But the damage is done between the time of mass infection and the time it fades away into obscurity. There the problem is what knowledge have the various pathogens & variants amassed between mass infection and fade and return.

.

Science fiction

It has been hundreds of years since the last Gemauglon onslaught. Which killed 750,000 people. But the world watches knowing that the multitude will not let the planet die an agonising death.

The planet is slowly receding from the sun and the effect on humanity with the cultivation of food looking good.

There is still devastation from tornadoes, hurricanes and earthquakes. Alas but weather is a fact of life. Without sustenance the land becomes unliveable.

Then a signal is received from an observatory on Guam in the pacific. They are here attacking. They have entered the atmosphere at 3 a.m. Pacific Meteorological Time (PMT).

There is millions rising from the sea and coming out of the sky. They have already reached the North-east side of the island. We have launched a pesticide contaminants but they keep coming. It is not if it is when they reach the mainland a famine will happen.

I do not know how long we can keep signalling. As you know containment means survival.

As the Gemauglon sweep across Guam, taking it out as if not there. The 5,000 populous are left in crippling dying agony.

Heading towards the mainland, waves from the sea begin to rise. The clouds in the sky begin to form into an ominous sight. Of grey and deep blue. Then a thunderous noise as like a lightning sweep strike. A terrifying sight for anybody in its way, as the Gemauglon reach land. They form an avalanche effect. Settling within months from continent to continent. With a paralyzing effect they come out of the Atlantic Ocean and perform there ritual of death (avalanche affect) across the western hemisphere. Then settling, humanity does what it knows best.

Empties chemists, initiates lockdown and starts sanitizing everything. A report comes in that there is something strange about the membranes. They are a deeper colouring than before. Two-half months later with death toll already at 500,000 it is reported that within the membranes there are multiple of contagion of the same pathogen., with different potency effect. So it is important that humanity reach-out for the antibiotics, vaccine for the gemauglon burst in their area.

It is important that they are denied sustenance. So as within decapitation can take place. It is now two-half years since and the loss of life (800,000,000) nearly three billion lives. Science reports that the infections are receding.

Six years later when something called normality settles in. It comes clear that unless the reasons for are extinguished. Then things shall continue to get worse. If the coauglons and the gemauglons are allowed to climatise the planet, there shall be no planet.

Sustenance and availability shall perish. So the planet shall wither away an become no more. Probability within seventy to hundred-seventy years.

WARNING the time-lock on space is not an earthly compound, there coming for you.

Compilation

Somehow the patient has been infected by a complete Gemauglon. Meaning the patient was within the realm of the Gemauglon membrane as it apartheid, and infection was easily sequenced.

As you see the patient is aligned to several different readers. Because of the different infections.

It is important that we monitor and control the infection spread, slowly trying to eradicate each disease. You will notice a strange factor that with the spread and blockage of each infected area. Temperature and vital signs seem to vary. We have put the patient on a flatline protocol. To enable the strengthening of the main arteries an organs. I want to stress how important it is to keep the patient alive. With twenty-four hour monitoring and surveillance. Take read-outs every ten minutes and log them out on the central computer.

Out there are many good people dying from the different surges. But this is our first multiple. If we come out on top and save the patient's life. Then we will take a great leap forward in forging an immune response.

Things are not looking good so we have to secede. It is important that we do so.

No person deserves what our patient is going through and as gone through.

Lumination

I have sent my mind deep into my mind, where now all I sense is emptiness. So now I am going to look at what shall be shall be.

Slowly I open my eyes and see a satellite with many antigens floating before. In a red colour.

Then a white blue circular shape with antigens starts floating forward out of the depths. Then a patch of red spots moving from left to right flashing on and off. Then patchy blobs appearing with a greyish colour in a stable position going on and off. After a while red spots appear randomly, then disappearing coming together in clusters. Then patchy blobs appearing in different shapes. In colours of red, grey and white yellow colour. Everything clears then I am seeing quakes of different levels of sand in the colour of gold and tinted in red.

Then bubbles floating around like balloons in clear light. Then a bright light getting brighter and brighter, then numbness.

Devotion to see without through covid-19, pneumonia, Leukaemia, Smallpox, Leprosy, Measles, Malaria, Polio. It is not to know it is to reach that window of safety.

Microbe

A gemauglon is formed when the influx of input does not equal the influx of output.

Where environment does not equalize with correct amount of sustenance. Where breathing and living begin to deteriorate. Creating a negative aroura in various atmospheres. So changes on mass take place in the micro environment.

The different particles which then have gone dormant evolve to come together. Because they are in the same movement of thought mode. To create a micro-organism come together, in a membrane of atmosphere.

Replicating billions of times over until reaching a protocol of infinite probability. Meaning to top heavy and probability equal survival. Where then the membrane divisions equal atmosphere survival and provocate. Where incubation recedes and the membrane does brake open. Then the instinct of life does begin.

With hunting and feeding are a purpose for to survive. This would repeat itself in a living reaction. Of purpose, finding and speed until desired purpose is reached. A desire for more sustenance for survival.

A coagulin is the same as above but the atmosphere is more equipped to provocate one kind of microbe.

It is an indispensable and mesmerising sight with the first encounters of life. A fundamental fact is how do you repeat when the act is performed and all of the knowledge of the process has been used.

Only dilapidation has a interfering sense in the progress of being.

MY (COVID-19) THESIS

WARNING this thesis has not been recognized
by any medical body or organization.

Now

The CDC in America is tracking a new variant of covid-19 called BA.4.6 identified in last days of July 2022, found in the state of Iowa, America. United Kingdom in August becomes first country to recognise omicron variant vaccine. Created by Moderna it can also protect against other variants. In September Pfizer introduce vaccine targeting omicron variant. On a passing note, the medical profession is using the word ' Bivalent ' for vaccines that particularly target variant omicron of virus. CanSino biologics inc, Tianjin, China given permission for use of inhaled vaccine to fight virus. In India Bharat Biotech (BBV154) Incovacc intranasal covid-19 vaccine given jurisdiction for use.

It is autumn, and the medical profession is pushing hard to stop the omicron variant of covid-19 with booster vacs and bivalent vaccinations. So far since the last virus surge the number of infections and deaths around the world has kept falling. Scientists say BA.4.6 is good at being evasive from the immune system.

E.U. justice department and home affairs agencies which has nine members. Have released two papers containing information on covid-19. In July 2020 and September 2022.

The WHO is now talking that the virus pandemic is now in its final phase.

P.S. Note: With so many diseases suddenly reoccurring it looks like the contagion is looking to creating super germs or covid become a super disease. Whatever, this new variant situation is moving at a dangerous incantation.

Scientists say when a new variant becomes dominant the former disappears a.k.a. dies. Or does it, is it not possible it goes into sleeper mode. As if waiting for a change in the directional surge?

P.S.S. Note: With so many variants would it not be possible to create a land base coviz plant. Then would not a water base coviz plant grown be a vaccine? Or would the growth create a coviz plant with the base being a vaccine, a.k.a. heavy water? Scientists in Canada claim they have created a plant vaccine.

Distorted

In the human anatomy there is something called the nervous system, which transports oxygen to breath. Acting as a reactor it sends reactions through different parts of the body.

Whereas the covid-19 antigen is a neuron network. Its main adversary is the lungs, with their distorting effect causing movement. When it blocks of the lungs it then tracks the anatomy reading of the brain signals through the nervous system to parts of the body. When it finds weak parts of the anatomy (because they cannot sustain a regular flow of oxygen). It blocks it off with rapid recuperation of virus. Because there are a large amount of cells with oxygen. There is a never-ending growth of antigens. Because no oxygen can get in the damaged part of the body dies. Thus, in many cases the whole body dies because the nervous system as broken down. Causing a chain reaction where blood cannot make or make enough plasma.

P.S. Note: Many scientists say when a variant of a virus dies its only possibility to survive is another variant taking its place. What if when a variant becomes de-energized it goes into a comma. So, when it awakens it is a fitter antigen. That makes the variant synonym wrong. It is really the same antigen awakening at a different energy level. Because you only see what is down your microscope can you catch the return from sleep mode. Where science comes to fore insure a closed environment. It is not covid-19 taking lives it is the human anatomy inability to survive.

Morpheus

Long covid, where the coronavirus symptom covid-19 is incomplete. Because the infection has forcibly been removed and not to float and withdraw. Where the infected has forcibly used oxygenised to eradicate the army of collapse. Or the infected has been forcibly feed oxygen to climatize the human Where it has been changed into a near death experience, with symptoms of wanting to die.

Meaning energy loss, slow to react, headache, pain, mental fatigue. Which are slowly coming together in aptitude because energy rises.

With the devastating problem for hundreds of millions. It would be good to surround yourself with close friends. When it hits walk, crawl, reach for the aspro, sleepers and hope for the best. It can and will come like a recurring nightmare if you are lucky.

I am mighty covitez, I am impenetrable. I stand alone as the only conqueror of some planet called earth. I come here as death; you ask who am I ? Then you will not have to ask any more. So you see where you can sense your existence. 'Without change you die' It is planet earth and all it see in you is nothing. Leave it to the intensity of the virus, stay stealth and survive. Your passing belief is just a reason you deserve a more torturous death.

P.S. Note : As the aroura of aroma float around the sleepy atmosphere of the place. An wide eyed you see what you want to see an look upon a wonder your fate is sealed.

Concern

The containment of covid-19 virus started in December 2019 has been very difficult. It has left people unsure if it will get worse or start to improve. It is now October 2022, and the numbers are and have been unfortunate around the world for all. With the virus now beginning to spread again. Official figures show in excess of 600,000,000 infected and 6,000,000 dead. The problematic problems of the virus do not seem to depicitating at present. But the knowledge of how to fight the disease has been producing different forms of antiviral medicines, (vaccines, nasal sprays, antibiotics). Because more is known about the virus effect. Countries are now learning how to live with the infection. The cost has been estimated in multi-billions.

With approximately over 200,000 people being infected per week it is far from eradicated. Though contamination has not been stopped. National security measures of countries have slowly been removed or made less stringent. Countries that can are still believing in a vaccine program (U.S., U.K., China). Symptoms of the virus are similar to other viruses and long covid remains a concern.

A statement has been made by the medical foundation that there are a greater number of deaths annually than is usual.

Sticky

These statements have been mentioned by science.

- Stress is a prediction of post-covid symptoms.
- Long covid is still a mystery.
- Does long covid cause blood clots.
- After three years there is still no standard treatment for long covid.
- For those with long covid it is a day to day problem.
- The procuring of omicron symptoms while ill is a mystery.
- Dose long covid hide something else.
- Those that caught omicron mostly did not realise.
- Why do symptoms change with each new variant.
- Some of those that have covid-19 think they shall never fully cover.
- Flashback and stress after having the virus is common.
- There are those having problems remembering things.
- The need for extra oxygen sometimes needed after recovered.
- Inability to return to work is common.

P.S. Note`: In the chasms of my mind I am not saying I understand the symptoms of long covid !

But as the covid wave came in creating nothing but chaos and terror. Then three years later because it is neurone network. They are rampant, so the terror it is creating is just you.

Because you are the host your mind has been taken over by the neurone network. Because your nervous system was and technically is still indisposed. In English trying to help you get on in life.

If my calculations are correct as you get tired, then the covid gets bored and gives it to,.

Meaning gifts you to another odds & sods.

So as not to interrupt the mission priorities as you are now a spy (survivor).

Some would say you should know, some would disagree. While the covid encampment is just out of reach. The warmth of the fire (you) is keeping them warm and energized. Wanting of more potency slowly but surely.

Until total boredom sets in and they swarm in a quickening to attack against what is opposite of your desire.

Dianoetic

In these deferential times, over the past three years. With the loss of so many lives and with so many, many more infected. From the infectious infection covid-19. We have been so very lucky to come through as we have so far.

It is hard to say what the future holds for the human race. But it must hold it together, not listen and allow domestic or international terrorism get the better of humanity.

I realise the scared are thinking that making the aware worse off sounds good. But that is not a safe and caring way to think in such a terrifying atmosphere. Going to war and making others weaker won't protect you from national fall-out.

The division in time should make humanity stronger if the human race is going to succeed in surviving. Belief in inadequacy and a life that does not exist anymore. Is not wanted and will fail leading to anarchy.

Truly pandemical.

Cheer-up

My fellow commanders of the fallen I would like you to know they show you no ill feeling.

For leaving them confused and then giving them the gift of a starving grieving diet.

They would also like to say that you're speeding up of giving your vaccine. That did not work and has caused only clandestine death and a weakening of their immune system. Is also unforgivable being forgivable seeing how upset they have been made.

As the liquidation of humanity through weakness and self-indulgence. The shadow effect of weakness an inexplicable ending of humanity is being handed out in a quickening effect. Which as so to forget the horror of coronavirus. The people of government shall just pronounce there is no cure for the unknown happening. The religious fanatics shall say. If you had nothing to prey for before, then you do now. Charities shall be saying we can't help you because of the collapse of the economy around the world. When protesters of the in clandestine murders are shot. Governments shall just say go home there is nothing for you here. As the pandemic surges in death and destruction. All terrorist activities in biological scenario's shall be found out and the insurgents shall be executed.

Starting again through suffering a search for a real vaccine. A search for a proper vaccine shall commence. That can stop, eradicate, and give humanity its right to life.

A strange image I have (shore) is that money shall be left to burn-out and coupons shall be the survival tactic. Excuse me I must have a drink of water as I explain. Then the stability of human survival slowly looks like it is calmly being able to be possible.

No this the innocence of I was placed on death row. Heck, this is the truth you terrorists shall be sorted out and eradicated from the face of the planet.

Whencever

So, it as finally come to this, as the flag is lowered to half-mast. Signalling the battle to commence. The two opposing armies of coronavirus, starved of energy approach each other. With the thought of devastation in their heart, mind, and eyes.

The two forces clash at the dawn of planet earth. As universal alignment is lost. The omicronize settle a difference that as long been thought of as shame. Devouring indifference to one another. The battle rages forth and the inevitable comes about. Where recombinant variants are created like an avalanche. The shield variants have nothing but tunnel vision. Searching out the false humans. Survivors that make claim to their fame and honour.

The battle like a blood bath changes from a dust storm to a mighty cloud. Standing on planet earth the pressure of the neurone wave is unleashed on the human mind, carriers. Forcing a splinter in the fabric of the earth. With the human and its nervous system being beguiled by the truth, shaking it to its core. The splinter in the planet crust increases in size. Into a never ending slowly growing divide.

As the variants adapt, the covis contingent begins to secede and recede as the planet brakes into two parts. One part ascending towards the sun. With the other towards float in space.

As the covitez rejoice in another victory in the rights of others. The standard is raised as all is sorted out. To all now destiny awaits the wonderment of the future.

What

President Biden of America has taken it in hand to say the covid-19 virus is over.

While China has again closed a major city of its country down because of a outbreak of covid-19 virus.

It is now the beginning of winter and the virus pandemic again as began to surge. Hospitals in U.K. are seeing a surge in patients and so have brought in mask mandates. Vulnerable people are being advised to get a covid-19 booster vaccination.

As the inquiry about the pandemic commences the incriminations about the handling of the pandemic are beginning to be handed around.

It is October 2022 and in India a new strain found in august of the covid-19 virus has been located. It has been called XBB also known as Gryphon & XBB.1 It is said to be very evasive of vaccines.

New variants BQ.1 & BQ.1.1 variants are causing a rise in covid-19 cases throughout U.S. and Europe. BF.7 variant found in Mongolia; China in January is spreading. BA.4.6 variant also known as Eterna found in U.S. steadily spreading.

For the first-time different variants of the omicron strain are prevailing in different parts of the world.

A news report on the airwaves have shown just how deadly it can be for science to play with virus pathogens. A Boston university science laboratory have created a hybrid version of the original covid SARS-CoV-2 virus. A cross between the original and omicron it is said to be more deadly. If so, the antigen change could lead to catastrophic consequences. Strict caution must be taken because quicker than, one could become one-billion and one. Because coronavirus kills oxygen particles. There has been a lot of mention of new cures against the covid-19 pandemic. But that has not stopped the resurgence of the virus this winter.

P.S. Note: Like an explosive splitting of the atom. Giving an insight into what could turn germicide into genocide.

Mind's Eye

I am sitting on the ground in a park. I look deep into my mind. I see a jumble of words, then the sentence. 'As in the beginning then shall be a end'. Then it clears an in a deep decent I descend into an Orb.

I begin to see the glimpses of words Delta, Omega, Alpha, Omicron, Omicron+. Then which seems a while I see Endine and Kodxtra.

Realizing they were reflects of the neurone of Covitez. With this now being an omicron plus phase then the end is but a phase of the beginning away. With that said then there is only one more phase that can happen. That being SARS-CoV-2 oblivion. Meaning Covitez is one meaning all.

This will contract a dramatic shock to the nervous system. Which will sense a feeling of death. Then a chill like sensation shall pass over the body. In the mind knowing only a wellness of body and mind got you through.

Then as the covis neurone cringes, what shall be is not. As is what was the beginning shall be the end. That is no more.

Enthralling

What a strange phenomenon to reckon that the Omicron covid variant (if true) as so many sub-variant and semi-variants. Then what would it be if the neurone energy variants came together.

If the science of what they are saying is true. What kind of energizing energy in the sub-variant forming as the omicron sub-variants mix back together. There in creating Omicron 2 (?). Or the original variant becoming one again. If that is true, then what did the energy form when it came part of again. Are you saying it is a stagnant connotation. Then what has become of the energy! Has it gone to make a foreign body called oxygen which humans crave.

Even if that is true, then are you saying the neurone effect will just create what was. Then from positive to negative omicron, do you know what you are developing. If you are correct then the energy of omicron would only better the energy evolvement of the dominant variants.

If this is true that would mean calculus of infection to death would half, magnitude of suffering would double. Those with infectious long covid would be in constant suffering until they died.

Then I am still returning to the idiocy of that is devised one as another. Does it make sense or is it still trying to scam the masses with unreal reaction.

Potionotics

A strange situation has arisen with the biological mishap in China. With the United Nations making the provocation of biological weapons a war crime and China abstaining. A serious mishap did occur in a laboratory in Wuhan, China. With such an explosive impact the Covis virus did in four months eat the oxygen supply of the whole of planet earth. Leaving humanity breathless, dead, and dying.

Now while waiting for the planet with the fairy people and supply carrying elves to re-introduce what they can. As humanity looked to be getting better.

Some terrorist state in a laboratory at a place called Boston in U.S.A. has gone against the amendment set forth by the United Nations. Which U.S. was renowned as the leader in calling biological weapons a war crime. Created a Covid of immense power. That has ripped throughout the world. Creating devastating variants of the Covis disease. Plus unleashed an Armageddon of a infection called respiratory surge virus (RSV). Which has been created by Covitez, fuelled by Influenza. All of which has been subjugated in less than two months.

Where one did go big another has gone bigger. From an explosion that was massive to a explosion of magnitude. The omicron 2 virus is a variant of magnitude which grows in magnitude. Which was a 80% death rate, 8 million mega cycle (24hr count), 8× / sq in.

Infectious dark matter which has no use for matter.

Where the perpetrators in China were rounded up and died on the way to prison from cyanide poisoning.

The terrorists in America were closely monitored and enticed with twenty million dollars being deposited in there bank account.

Then to ensure the success, they were given the formulation. To how the mice will live and die, offering an 80% chance. Saying, okay it is up to you. For the furverment of science, think of the achievement Where are they now! That is a lot of money, anyway it told you for the advancement of science.

P.S. Note: With it being true or false it is a step forward then two steps backward. Where science is a world of discovery. This dilemma has taken it to another level. Is there time, only what is left.

Onward

Though different variants of the covid-19 infection have been found in different parts of the world. They are now beginning to spread with BQ.1 & BQ.1.1 variants being found in India. BQ.1 also identified as BA.5.2.1.7 variant. XXB a recombinant variant dubbed Gryphon first found in Singapore called nightmare is no worse than other subvariants scientists say. Has been found in U.S. & U.K. and New Zealand. The BF.7 variant is spreading in U.S.A. & Europe. The BA.4.6 variant dubbed Aeterna is slowly gaining in infection rate.

BA.2.75 found in U.S. May 2022 and BA.2.75.2 subvariant dubbed Centaurus.

Scrabble is a nickname given to variants that use letter B, X, or Q.

Adapted vaccines are being issued. They are vaccines that are tweaked to better resist infection from circulating variants of covid-19 virus. The Spikevax bivalent vaccine was approved in September 2022. They also give protection against original SARS-CoV-2 strain.

Scrable variants are appearing extensively around the planet and are said to be highly immune evasive. With BQ.1.1 showing greatest spread ability. Another variant of concern is BA.5.2.6 identified in Ukraine.

There is a concern from around the world. As Hospitals in U.S.A. are being converged on with 'Tripledemic', Flu, Covid-19, RSV (respiratory syncytial virus).

Around the world there are now different types of variants with their related problems.

P.S. Note: RSV is very infectious to children. It effects the lungs in breathing. Causes fever, tightening of skin, high temperature.

It is the dread of the unknown where omicron is depleted to its invisible beginning.

Syncytial

As the fallout from the new wave of covid-19 variants continues.

The respiratory syncytial virus (RSV) pandemic is spreading from its first encounter in New York city U.S.A.

With the reaction occurring in an energy form from covid, flu, cellular obstruction, virus. It is spread from droplets containing the virus. Through coughs and sneezes. It can survive on surfaces for a few hours and on your hands for a shorter time. Can be spread by touching a contaminated surface.

The infection can last for three to eight days in children and those with weakened immune system. The infection can still be spread even if a person shows no symptoms. For up to four weeks.

Symptoms are Runny nose, Coughing, Fever, Sneezing, Wheezing, Loss of appetite.

There is no vaccine at present. Those infected should isolate at home. Cover their mouth and nose when coughing.

Definition of Syncytial: A large cell like structure formed by the joining together of two or more cells.

P.S. Note: The fallout of inadequate measures taken with covid-19 has become clear.

Will the antidote to the consequences be a mass fire of living burn out.

It is very clear that you should teach yourself to do proper. With the truth you are faced with.

Is RSV the contagion or can its effect become more contagious. Meaning can it hype up its degree of infectiousness.

Inspect

It is now November 2022 and concerning the atrocity of procuring biological infectious variants. By insinuating that it was a accidental finding when they created a synthetic covid-19 variant. The science at Boston university U.S.A. is already trying to cover their tracks. Which is a sign that the experimentation and dossier of said find is disappearing or has mysteriously disappeared.

Which has brought into focus the RSV epidemic as was it caused by a synthetic covid collaboration or was it a natural covid transformation. Whatever it was an whatever the fake news. The procuring of a biological nuclear synthesis is beyond the laws of living. Which was clearly a terrorist act. If they clearly concentrated so hard in their experiment.

Did, they detect a .025 drop in synthesis of the variant to procure an antigen of decimation. If no, they were found out in time. But if so, are you saying that you couldn't believe the ferocity of its destructive out-take.

I see we have a problem here, you cannot contain covitez. It will energise and obliterate through the containment.

What I am seeing here is you did try to do such a thing. So, you are covering your tracks by injecting a human thought process. That devastative annihilation are you now starting to read the process of what you did. Or have I got you sweating your guts out if someone asks you questions.

Whatever, the moments are deceminating from time of origin. Questions shall be asked who the leader is, names, where did you get your funding, did you inform anyone, were you given permission to use university grounds, was it university equipment used.

Then there shall be important scientific queries. Such as how long did experiment take, did your synthesis and if so before or during experiment. How long after the joyous moment did you suddenly realise you had lost control and had to report it to the authorities.

Lost in the expediential intrigue of my mind I must warn you.

Do not try to give me any gibberish. That you had to do it, or you do not understand. You will not be able to contain, and those antigens must not be plexed to a false reading. The facts are clear how easy it is to manipulate with the words 'okay if you do not want'. In the eyes of truth and you are found out it shall be you that will be considered the terrorist not them.

Spymaster

Agent Zip your here good, things are getting heck-tick so would you please bring us up to date with the situation so far.

Certainly, in December 2019 in the city of Wuhan in China a problem did arise. With an outbreak of coronavirus, which after exploitation the name was changed to covid-19. The scientific name being SARS-CoV-2. Then within 4 months the epidemic changed to a pandemic. Having spread over the whole planet. Then climatizing itself the virus split into different deadly variants. Namely Beta, Gamma, Omega, Delta and Omicron.

The first named did evolve into being deadly pathogens in their own right. Killing and infecting countless millions. Whereas the omicron variant did split into tens of different sub-variants. Though being called a weaker strain. Because of its varying antigen sequencing it was still able over time to kill and infect many of humanity.

There is now a problem with waning vaccines. Which after a few months a booster shot is required. Then with some variants being able to avoid detection from the immune system infection becomes a greater danger. Also, some variants are very infectious, making it easier to spread the virus.

A massive danger has arisen in that at a laboratory in Boston, Massachusetts, U.S.A. Scientists have created a synthetic covid that is 80% deadly. Which is a mirror image of the dominant variants which so far have killed many.

Spymaster #2

Please bear with me to understand this I have gone deep undercover. At the end of the second world war. There evolved the most dangerous place on earth. A place called Wuhan in China. Where a very sophisticated laboratory of biological science was commissioned. To evolve a partial beginning from pi. A particle compound from the beginning of was composed. There upon bombarded with the aroura of atoms.

There then upon doing so it unknowingly created a rising energy force which found connection with all earth quantity. From bit by bit, until it was stuffed. Where then in an instance it saw dominance of planet earth and took it. Knowing the fact, it killed oxygen it was a easier fact to conquer the planet.

Seeing the environment it created in the atmosphere at the peak of its infection was something I had not seen since the 1960, s. The biggest and greatest cause of humanities quadrium was the searching effect and finding that human beans at the final end had nowhere to go. So, to be endorsed with an eventual ending.

P.S. Note: Any knowledge of the above shall be denied by the corni consortium.

As an unequivocal and inexplicable lie!

Dedication

Bestowing to, from coronavirus. Now that is out the way. Let the journey begin. As the fish market in the dingy, seedy part of town has a slow day flogging the trout. To explain the want of a human it is necessary to wonder in the past and bring it to the fore. As alexander the great falls sick from polio and it is explained that he is not going to live to enjoy his treasure. When Julius Caesar made claim to empire. Has the knife penetrated to kill him it told him he was going to be put down with cholera for wanting. When Genghis khan finished building the biggest empire ever known on planet earth and was about to anoint it with sex, did he cometh upon and died from smallpox within two days. Whereas Attila the Hun grovelling in all his glory listening to his court of wise men. Did suffer and die before the week was out from pneumonia. Where when there was Adolf Hitler who amassed himself, a fortune then died from typhoid with it just out of his grasp.

Has the human now sees the partial exploration to a new beginning. Rising from its past life into the endeavour of the unknown.

Struggling pursuing any which way it can to rise above the situation. From any which way and when what shall be the wonderous outcome that awaits.

Cocktail

It is now November 2022 and the SARS-CoV-2 aka Coronavirus aka Covid-19 virus is now seemingly entering a new phase.

From what were known as dominant variants at the beginning of the pandemic. To the Omicron strain. Which was spread from partial omicron to the next partial omicron Varying month to month around the world. Then in October 2022 various variants of different aptitude began to show, at the same time around the world. Which came to be known as the Scrabble variants. Basically B,Q,& Z signeas. Which are referred to as a cocktail of variants.

Given the nicknames Gryphon, Centurion, and Nightmare.

The strain system has still not divided from being called part of the omicron variant.

Which looks very suspiciously like taking a symptom and making it a name for a variant.

Which has made the genome look farcical of the truth of what is and where is SARS-CoV-2 going.

Example saying Coronavirus caused RSV just because you have made it ' said ' everything it is not. Where it just looked like you have scrambled ' damaged ' the sequencing so bad you cannot say if it is the virus or not.

So what are you saying when someone dies you can say it is the virus because you say so after manipulating someone's genome. Where subtracting the purity of a medicine to baseline it as a virus base so it is the virus.

With what you are doing then you are looking for another dominant variant. They will be spreading around the planet before you find them.

Another subject of the undoing of DNA sequence is all the injections ' vaccines ' you say people must take into their bodies. So, you do not think you are making the immune system inoperable! Changing its antigen abilities around to understand all the different virus antigens. Especially now you say the new virus variants are immune evasive. So, what do they do to the immune system when they attack it. Has the biological clock started going backwards (DNA).

It does not make sense the need of so many injections when all is needed is one or two. With all this immune system change if a proper vaccine is found. Will there be any immune system left to understand it? Will the vaccinated (before) body except the vaccine? Where a proper vaccine is usually a instant immune effective response. With ending of infection from planet or at least 90% protected against. What is the thinking that eradication of the evolution of vaccine efficacy is good.

Sodin heck

I am a bad man, no don't say that! I will prove it to you. I am walking through a petrified forest. You know how you think something is crawling over you. Well, that is what it feels as it is happening. It is a sense of slow scariness to out of your mind.

Firstly it feels all corni as if everything is falling apart. It is a slow repeated shock with the terror that there is nothing that can be done about it.

Then as if desperation as got hold changing becoming a vaccine junky. But it keeps fading out destroying resistance to the horridness. As like awakening to a bigger beast than before.

Now being possessed by the beast like a disease. It is slowly as picking up speed leading to an end. A sense of looking on it show certain death. So, like in an infestation so be it and then come out of it maybe.

Like a mad man it comes upon you blame the venom for everything. They believe this so easy as they should believe that. So, their dying does not know what you're on about. Besides cost too much so what can I do.

Sensing in the mind., thinking it is here. The night of a thousand knives has arrived. While sensed all around do not let them know you are you. Because they are coming. If they get you, they shall gorge upon with nothing to stop them. It is the dawn of the soup variation. Then thinking what is! When all your worldly fears rip you apart. Then the sense of emptiness before nothing.

With the terrifying truth of humanity reminding you that the variant is going to be with the human race for a while. With no permanent stopping of its ferocity.

Then when all is said and done, Will filling you with cures that fail and mixing-up the immune system until it goes dormant, all it come out with dose not make sense, or it say one thing then the opposite, or just an out an out lie. Then it gloats about it! Now all that is left is to heck with its petrifying.

P.S. Note: Will the persistence of the washed up past live to survive the onslaught. Will the persistence of the next generation survives.

Who is to know when it is death to you all.

Revamp

Presently the planet is going through a dangerous phase of the covid-19 pandemic.

These are my understanding of the present situation.

With the new variants which are said to be immune evasive. A small problem is slowly growing to become a big problem. With the virus working as a neurone network created by anti-matter. A very dangerous force has awoken with the scrabble variants.

E.g., XXB, BQ.1 With them being immune evasive they are beginning to spread at a expediential speed. To being able to say they are from another dose not give a connection of how they have been able to spread. A thought is with the science being able to get out of control, the experimental covid-19 bomb created in a Boston, U.S.A. laboratory. Has had a lot to do with the awakening of the scrabble variants, the creation of BQ.1 & BQ.1.1 and the creation of the RSV infection. Which are spreading and putting a strain on health systems around the world.

Because of the repetitive count it does not look like it will be long before a new deadly coronavirus is found. Which will have a highly toxic effect on the human anatomy. Which because of the disregard of the danger of splitting a covid-19 cell. Will not be realised until it as spread and is well established on the planet.

With the braking down of the covid-19 virus. The effort of destabilising its ability has had a opposite effect. Where sleeping through the so-called changes, it is now able to read and de-activate the immune protectorate. To carry on with its purpose. Using energy that has been lying dormant and is now re-directed.

Until there is no hindering properties from outside sources.

.

Ranges

It is now November 2022 and A sub-variant XBB.3 of Omicron found in India. XBB is a easily spread recombinant lineage between two sub-lineages. Also being watched is variant BA.4.6 Scientists are now watching a resurgence of Deltacron's. With ability to infect lungs like Delta variant and quickly spread like Omicron variant. They are XBC Philippines variant, XAY South Africa variant and XAW Russia variant.

China with its zero tolerance and lockdowns is facing a difficult time with various variants causing infection and with people trying to leave. Reporting the worst infection rate in six months. Violence has broken out across China because of the zero tolerance against the Sars-CoV-2 virus.

With what is called live with the virus. Countries are slowly withholding daily data. Such as daily infection rate and death rate. The stopping of free vaccinations. The true conditions in constituencies. The seriousness of the latest effects. Dangers of decomposing a variant when not understanding what they do.

E.g. a cold or cough is the disease... People are questioning what is being reported about the spread !

A new wave of the virus is occurring in China, Australia and America.

New variant BN.1 found in U.S. is very effective at resisting vaccines, but is of a mild infection capability. It has been found also in other countries e.g. Australia, India. Because of all the new variants with the capability to evade immune efficacy. Hospitals are running out of antibiotics to affect a cure for patients. Of the new variants BQ.1 & BQ.1.1 are the most prevalent in U.S.A. The new soup variants are now dominant around the world. BBX, BQ.1, BQ1.1, BF.7

Variant BW.1 which is evasive against immune efficacy has been found in Mexico.

Simpleton

I am flatlining and something is messing with my time-line. So I am going to enact emergency protocol. As the on mass biological warhead is exploded in China. The virus as enacted on mass annihilation of the humanity on the planet.

With its first act being to engulf China and turn the populous into a viral time-bombs.

Then using the silk road it did mask its existence in conquest of the third world. By promising nothing would happen to the camels. It then did slowly spread about the third world.

Then it did unleash an attack on the Northern and Western hemisphere.

Then rising from fusion of simpleton and flatliner, then creating a welcoming committee of want of this or that. Or then what about that or this. So as it forged through the barrier it was to late it has happened.

As the west was attacked it did explode the time-bomb reaction. Which has now after almost three years engulfed the far pacific of China to Australia and heading towards New Zealand.

When the explosion reaches its peak and begins to subside it will only be the dividing factor to stand against the virus. The energy levels of the virus will not recede until it is tired. After it reach the pinnacle of attack process.

P.S. Note : It is dangerous to talk about what you would do if another contagion did occur when we are in a pandemic process.

It is not easy to devise between the things that have been said and done. Which have had a negative effect. Preparedness is the only factor of safety before an infection strike. When is a diagnosis and after the fact is what is good in case of a next time.

Topography

In December 2019 the virus Sars-CoV-2 which came to be known as Covid-19 was discovered in Wuhan, China.

From China the virus spread throughout Asia and Africa into Europe. From Europe it spread to Russia, U.S.A. and then Latin America.

While coming down harshly around the world. It did not affect India and Africa badly until it had spread around all of planet earth.

While the rest of the world was badly infected China and the far pacific Australia & New Zealand got off lightly.

In November 2022 Australia was affected by a new surge. Then in December 2022 China started suffering very badly from the virus surge. What the rest of the planet has been suffering the past three years. China and the far pacific is only just beginning to feel the horrific consequences of the pandemic.

The strange factor is that the virus that started in China is now only beginning to feel the harsh effect of the pandemic surge. From a zero tolerance of the infection then immune evasive variants, with its spread into the far pacific. It is going to suffer a terrible rush on medicine and intense pressure on its medical foundation. Not forgetting the terrible suffering of so many people.

A problem that is evolving to be a problem to the whole planet. Is the fact that the new variants are benign immune evasive. Then there is the waning vaccines and the ability of the disease to spread much more rapidly, led by the BBX variant.

Productial

It is now December 2022 and China has relaxed sanctions against Covid-19 following mass protests in the country.

With variants immune to the vaccine efficacy dominant around the world and waning vaccines. The stability against the spread of covid-19 looks questionable. A massive covid bomb has unleashed in the far pacific extending from China to Australia with New Zealand expecting to be engulfed by the surge.

Strange words spoken by science, that the covid-19 virus can live on food for days. Then does that mean the pathogen is gaining cannibalistic tendencies ! Science is again out of place. Just because it is not after the fact it is making different negative assumptions.

E.g. it is a bad omen with China dropping its zero covid-19 policy, another surge is coming, WHO claim it is not right to think the virus is finished. Why cannot such statements be said when they occur ! Human endeavour has the right to react to facts not unknown data.

It has been found that a new variant BF.7 , an immune evasive variant is most transmissible in Beijing, China. It is a sub-linage of BA.5.

A new list of variants are BR.2.1 and XBF originating in Australia. Other variants found around the planet XAS, DJ.1, DJ.1.1, CM.2.1, CJ.1, BE.9, BF.2.6, BQ.1.1.2, BZ.1

The sig variant classification used to monitor the virus is :

(A) Variant being monitored (VBM).

(B) Variant of interest (VOI).

(C) Variant of concern (VOC).

(D) Variant of high consequences (VOHC)

Since China abandoned its zero covid stance a wave of the virus is engulfing the nation. With crematoriums stretched to the limit difficult times lay ahead. Many people now free to travel from China are at their final destination being found to have covid-19. So countries are tightening their entry requirements from China. Drugs are in short supply, hospitals are overwhelmed. Surge of virus expected to last until April 2023.

Various worrying symptoms are being found such as covid-19 infection in the lungs and being found in the brain.

P.S. Note : Now that the virus has completed the evolution of the planet. What enactment will take place next ? Will there be a reversal surge for another three years of turmoil or will the soup kitchen effect take place. Where variants of continents shall stay and eat humanity alive until dead. Then there is the double effect of one at a time or both together.

Whatever ! The virus effect is highly contagious incarnate mainly in the far pacific for now.

Bubba

Here is a list of the problems which have occurred in China since December 2022. When the zero covid-19 precautions were lifted.

Mass rapid infection of the populous.

Reports of self-infecting.

Thousands dying daily.

Drugs to fight virus non-existence or in short supply.

Medical staff having to work, though infected.

Many staff are exhausted.

China rushes to build temporary hospitals.

Hospitals over crowded.

Patients being taken care off outside hospital.

Sick patients lying on floor waiting for a bed.

No hospital beds available for those that are sick.

Long line ups at funeral parlours, bodies piling up.

Some cremation burials taking place in the streets.

Relatives having to take dead loved ones to be cremated.

Body bags, shrouds, coffins, urns, wreaths running out.

Shops in the cities empty and no shoppers on the streets.

Factories struggling to keep going, with employees phoning in sick.

Mail deliveries pilling up at sorting depots.

Chinese nationals are renewing their passports and leaving the country.

Other countries putting entry restrictions on Chinese nationals.

Many prominent people and officials are being reported dead.

Scammers are out and about.

Economy spiralling out of control because of virus, lay-offs, riots and demonstrations.

Banks are collapsing.

Variants of the virus are being found in China that are nowhere else in the world.

Because of the land mine effect as it generates around the country every person in China will be infected. As the energy of the virus bomb perspires upwards towards its pinnacle of its extremities. When it capitulates and energizes in a downward spiral. The fall-out will have a devastating affect for Indo-China, Korea, Oriental isles, Australia and New Zealand. Then the fold will be complete, thus expecting the virus to float in a new world search for a neurone negative effect.

Expecting the virus to capitulate and just give up is hard to expect. When you consider how dominant and immune evasive the new variants are. Because of how deadly the outbreak is in China countries are closing there boarders to China. So it is going to be a slow manipulating effort of the medical profession to get the infected back to health again, and caring people to help slow the spread of the infection. A major obstacle is the immune evasive variants to be able to infect where they will and so quickly. Where one infected person can infect 18 to 22 persons in a twenty-four hour period. The symptoms of the virus is a big concern. With symptoms of white lung infection, brain infection, growing of abnormal hair, quickening of ageing process. XBB.1.5 symptoms of fever, Diarrhoea and vomiting are causing chemists to run out of medicines. Countries around China will be scrambling to ensure they have a supply of vaccines available. Which with a mass exodus from China and the fall-out they shall certainly be needed. China stubbornness with not giving a true account of the situation and withholding the death count. Then refusing help from outside its borders is a worrying sign to the rest of the world. With request coming from WHO for clarification and E.U. offering vaccines being denied.

A prominent physician in China has come out and said that the clinical care in China hospitals does not work. Re-infections are prominent and seriously dangerous.

With the effect of the virus exploding causing an infection then energizing causing a white lung effect. Is it possible that it is a camouflage enactment to create a covid-19 bomb. Thus enacting the destruction of China and the fall-out infecting the rest of the planet with the body bag effect ?

As the 'r' number goes from 18 to 22 in China what can the world expect to receive ! Is China going to be the first nation to discover the super vaccine against the virus ? Then stop the terrifying death manipulating energy of the covitez onslaught. It's true or are they going to count themselves to dead, at the expense of country folk !

Panic is setting in China with the virus reaching outlying areas and mountainous villages. With many reports of dead love ones.

.

Time

It is now January 2023, which is now three years since the virus covid-19 started spreading. I am not going to mention the number of casualties or deaths. Because many countries are no longer reporting accurate data.

The epee centre of the virus is in China and the winter surge is beginning to fluctuate round the world. A new variant called XBB.1.5 has begun spreading rapidly around U.S.A. and is spreading in other countries. It is highly immune evasive and can connect more quickly to body cells. Has been given the name Kraken variant.

A serious symptom being caused by the virus covid-19 in China is white lung infection. Which is damage to the lungs, which re-generates in cycle of infection and causes pneumonia, resulting in many people dying. It is the XBB & BF.7 variant that is causing the mass infection of life in China. As the land mine effect is epidemic in concentration across the country body bags are pilling-up across the country.

Other nations are checking visitors from China, but finding no new variants.

Japan is reporting a eight wave of the virus has begun, with thousands dying just last month. With a record number of deaths in the first week of January of 400+. Hospitalizations are rising around the planet, is this the beginning of the wave effect after China collapses and then begins to improve. Scientists are rushing to find a way to try and stop the fast infecting and immune evasive variants as they are spreading unchecked around the world. These variants are climatic death throws that will cause untold damage.

A new variant CH.1.1 has been detected in India. It has a Delta mutation which worries scientists.

There are four variants of concern in China they are BA.5.2, BF.7, XBB, XBB.1.5 . It is chaos with medication in short supply, Funerals on mass with new incinerators quickly being erected. There are queues of coffins waiting for cremation. Price of burial very high. Many privately performed cremations taking place. People desperate to leave and outsource virus medications. Many home sourced meds are being found as fake. There is problems with energy supply requirements

Another variant CA.3.1 found December 2022 in U.S.A. and considered highly infectious. Japan has reported its first death count of over 10,000 since pandemic began.

P.S. Note : A strange phenomenon to observe is the deteriorating annihilation of the Chinese. Then the after effect being a time-bomb for the rest of the world. Caused by the fall out of the devastation.

Horrendous

China is in a desperate fight for life with this just being the first wave of the virus covid-19 since China lost out to the virus surge. If there is no change it is predicted by December 2023 there will be around 12,600,000 dead. Whatever the reading it is important that the Chinese people keep it together and preserve their right to existence.

Chances of survival will keep plummeting and will only level out when it find that connection. Which is connecting to the flatline synopsis what I first observed as closest to the chance of survival when the rest of the world was in the grip of death. Before assurity of survival kicked into the human intellect it took another two months before the populous were reassured. Where there is no hope just phooy you must keep it together and preserve your right to exist. Humanity is in a desperate state of mind. They are part of the human faction and in the eyes of the world if China dies so do they. People are falling down unexpectedly everywhere from virus infection. Does that mean China is moving from annihilation to extinction ?

How deadly is a virus variant that can infect a country the size of China in one month.

Are the variants sleepers (land- mine) stature. Working the neurone network to explode together ? If so will they survive or will the cannibal aspect win through ? With the immune evasive variant CH.1.1 now in China it is getting hard to distinguish between influenza and the covid-19 virus. When you figure that the virus just piggy backs on the very contagious influenza virus. Creating a infiltration destruction process of the anatomy.

This was a provocative and despicable act by the covid-19 neurone network to ensure the annihilation of China for the next generation.

The covid-19 landmine effect turning into a bomb is having a devastating effect on China.

The Chinese are trying to escape into the future by saying the first wave is over and a second surge is coming. No data coming out of China is compatible with the facts. Of packed hospitals and line-ups at morgues to cremate the dead.

Western investors are in a desperate push to leave China as its economy fractures.

Also Chinese people are beginning to lose faith in the China way of life and large numbers are trying to leave the country.

Western propaganda is rife saying China a country in an epidemic emergency is the aggressor. With sanctions being attempted by the west.

Whatever the facts in all forms of existence China looks to be deteriorating.

.

Hope & Phooy

Hello, folks just to let you know you have not been forgotten.

It is just the terror ripping through China, the place must feel like it does not know whether it is coming or going. Let us hope after the first wave of mass died. They get a better understanding of the situation. It looks and seems both terrible and heart-breaking for them all.

So what about India claiming only hundreds of thousands died. Then WHO saying the number is closer to thirty-five million. Then in U.S.A. saying they have one million died. Then the CDA saying the real number is closer to twenty million. The U.S. government then saying that Brazil is running a close second to them.

Then we have China where western propaganda does not exist. Meaning a source saying 60,000+ died, then the official figure 5000+.

What can you believe except for the horror you see in hospitals, the loss of loved ones to the virus covid-19, or your own experience in coming down with said infection.

Who do you believe a nurse that tells you that aka scientists are no closer to a cure. Or all the exerts from the internet !

So if my calculations are correct we have hope aka life, phooy aka how good waning vaccines are and weirdness aka the terrible effect the virus has on the human anatomy.

So we mix them all together in a cauldron and it's got to be fairly good surely !

.

Yes & No

In 2004 the Sars virus was found in bats, then in 2009 the Mars virus was found in cows farm livestock. Then we had covid-19 in humans. Which is why some science think that the virus was passed from animal to human. Mars, Sars and Covid-19 are all part of the coronavirus sect.

Then there is the science that say covid-19 came from trout fish to humans. Where fish are not technologically animals.

There is much talk that other animals have caught the coronavirus, e.g. Mink, Deer, Tiger.

Which is not covid-19 which devastated humanity.

Now lost in thought science has returned to the biological science laboratory theory.

Mainly the cause of covid-19 the science laboratory in Wuhan, China. Where scientists have made claim they have been plagiarizing DNA in dangerous format. To back-up the theory science at Boston university, Massachusetts, U.S.A. claim to have created a synthetic covid-19 virus. We then had the manipulation of the spread of bivalent of covid-19, starting in America.

The neurone network of the virus is again leaving human aspect to talk and die. Of the human affects that made the virus covid-19.

P.S. Note : Whatever humanity does to make claim. The virus is making bivalent changes through-out its evolvement. Whereas difficulties for humanity keep mounting. Throughout the pandemic science say so has been left lagging in its knowledge in what it has discovered.

Science seems to be leading to the forefront of its knowledge. That is to know but have no answers. Where waning vaccines and interfering science is creating more danger than creating a safety factor.

Informed

Hello, G,day, Hi, this is an informal prompt going out on universal broadcast on zero megahertz.

Over the past three years I have been collecting data on the covid-19 virus. This is the petrifying read-out conclusion I have configured.

With the climate change we are now registering with days getting warmer and catastrophic anomalies in the weather. The planet is slowly becoming uninhabitable and is being sucked into the sun. Where it will shrivel into particle sun ions.

This discriminate annihilation of humanity by the covid-19 virus and weather anomalies is to destabilize the earth's axis. So it will drift away from the sun. By purifying the atmosphere and give the sun less potential to burn. To accomplish such a feat the topography of the planet shall have to change. All this shall happen within 100 years. As the planet population reaches 10 billion where it is unable to accommodate or feed such a vast number. Where temperatures shall sore and the air shall be taken out of the atmosphere if the planet does not start retracting from the sun.

Your concerns shall be met by the amalgamation of covid-19 and the climate with warmth from within. A liveable atmosphere must and shall be acquired for humanities sake. The amount of degree of planetary change is depending on the viable commodity of space to be able to accommodate the earth.

Indifference

— Virus can be caught from dead bodies
— The virus can be active on food
— Can cause growth hairs on tongue
— Stuffy nose or runny nose
— Nausea
— Inability to stay awake or awaken
— Inconsistency in breathing
— Dry itchy throat
— Problematic in speech
— Brain fog
— Congestion
— New confusion
— Lack of desire to do things
— Feeling blues
— Fever 39°C
— Chilly but sweating
— phlegm appears
— Loss of appetite
— Feeling or being sick
— Persistent pain or pressure on chest
— Pale grey, or blue skin tone, lips, Nail beds
— Flat rash covered in small bumps
— Swollen discoloured fingers or toes
— Light sensitivity, sore eyes, itchy eyes
— Hyposomnia, sleep deprivation
— Black tongue

— Constant desire for food

— Persistent crying

F.T. Note : The virus has been showing new signs of infection as new variants have evolved. Symptoms can appear 2 to 14 days after infection and range from mild to severe, can cause death.

With so many different symptoms the strain on the immune system could be the effect of long covid. Or the virus is causing a parallax obscuring some virus symptoms from view, creating a mini immune deficiency.

Is humanity unknowingly creating a super solvent to resolve humanities obstinacy in living in an impossible environment.

Devils & Angels

Before we find out about the angels. I would and feel devoted to letting you know about the devils.

As the world perishes from a pandemic and the dead have become a menial number.

A so called vaccine is given out to the world, then told it does not hold its efficacy. The profit to vaccine companies is in $ Billions.

The side effects of said vaccine are death or near-death experience. From heart attack, blood clot, oxygen deprivation. Another such problem is the rumour that the pandemic is the cause of massive prices for food and living essentials. Especially when their yearly profits are in the record $ billions. For something that cost pittance to develop. Where the latest word is blaming the war in Europe, in some place called Ukraine.

Another dangerous outtake of greed is the persistence of trying to enforce the right to international travel. With business & holiday travel. When it is just enhancing the virus situation. You have created an atmosphere of financial security which cannot exist. While growing steadily it will show its worth as nothing.

Then to devise and manipulate the truth shall be the only way to reach survival.

Now that lot is over, I would like to give a mention the angles of this world. The good doctors and nurses. Though getting ill themselves, those that survived did return to their duties to help the unfortunate. The charity workers that did tirelessly give their time to give food and supplies to the deprived.

Then there are the good neighbours who did show compassion to others. Giving help when requiring supplies or surviving.

P.S. Note: Where the virus is bound is clear. It has attacked and destroyed. It is now trying to escape into the future. To prepare for worse.

The truth of what to do shall be written in the past.

Statutorial

- Regular exercise could help with effectiveness of vaccines.
- Omicron variants are a threat to people with immune deficiencies.
- SARS-CoV-2 shows signs of genetic engineering.
- Covid-19 boosters reduce chance of infection.
- Covid-19 virus will run out of steam.
- Different covid variants show different symptoms.
- The symptoms depend on which strain of the virus.
- The next deadly strain of covid-19 will be called Pi.
- Where the omicron strain dose not compare to the strains of covid-19 before it. Deadly activation of virus is coming.
- New complications & challenges arise because of virus variant changes.
- A study in covid-19 genomic (waste water) research showing new insight.
- Omicron sub-variant BA.4.6 can evade immunity and might cause re-infection.
- Latest omicron sub-variants can infect those that have had covid-19 virus.
- Vaccine market failures will hinder us in next pandemic.
- So many different omicron variants suggest big wave is coming.
- Nations are monitoring spatiotemporal spread of covid-19. Recoveries, Dead, Effects of partial and full vaccination.
- Vaccine roadmap (Uni Minnesota U.S.) being prepared against future pandemics.

- Gotten covid, then symptoms might depend on vaccination status.
- Population growth is falling
- Booster vaccinations reduce chance of infection.
- Rapid rise in immune evading covid variants.
- Adjuvanted Novavax booster adapts to new variants.
- A bigger covid booster uptake needed to quell outbreak of disease.
- It is a mystery why some people get the virus and others never do.
- People with mild covid had a higher chance of getting blood clots.

Vision of Folded- Space

I would like to give a big thank you to all those that have helped in the publishing of my book.

Also thank you to those that found the time to read my book, I hope you found it interesting.

Whatever the future holds for humanity instigations shall be the forefront of survival.

By Keith Radmall

If I am in pain I shall get through it!

Uptake : Space exploration is a slow process of development and procedure.

War is a grievance with far reaching consequences.

Anti-matter is the total opposite to human survival, so mess with it then you are either lucky or suffer unto yourself.

www.ingramcontent.com/pod-product-compliance
Lightning Source LLC
Chambersburg PA
CBHW020342220726
48290CB00013B/530